瑞蘭國際

瑞蘭國際

搭配詞的力量
THE POWER OF COLLOCATIONS

動詞篇

序

在當老師前，我就是個把語言學得很好的學生。

但一開始只是自我「感覺」知道怎麼學得好，直到後來學習到第二語言習得（Second Language Acquisition），我才知道原來「怎麼樣能把語言學得最好」是個可以用科學研究的議題，也開啟了我對語言學習科學的認識。

在學習過程中，影響我特別深的，是一位叫韓照紅（ZhaoHong Han）的中國籍女教授。認識她的人，包括很多學界的教授，都知道她講話鏗鏘有力，授課風格極為嚴格且犀利。讓對知識有真熱情的學生，修習她的課程如入寶山。「What is teaching?」、「How do you know if your students are really learning?」10 年過去了，她在哥倫比亞大學 Grace Dodge Hall 的教導言猶在耳。

對於精通中文、英文、日文，也曾經粗淺地學習過法文的我，她曾經跟我談到，藉由眾多學習語言的經驗，我會有更多更準確的「直覺」（stronger intuition），知道可能什麼才是較正確的學習語言方法，而我們可以再去用實證研究驗證那些直覺。也就是在研究第二語言習得的過程當中，我認知到了「chunking」（語塊）的概念的重要性。

眾多認知心理學研究顯示，我們的大腦，相對於「離散」（discrete）的資訊，對於記憶一塊有連結性、有系統的資訊群比較在行。而「collocations」（搭配詞）的學習，即是因應大腦這樣的特性。同時也可以讓我們在思考字和字如何搭配使用時，防堵我們的「中文腦」滲透進去。搭配詞就是一個詞組，而這個詞組裡

頭可能包含兩個甚至兩個以上習慣搭配在一起的字（A collocation is a familiar grouping of words, especially words that habitually appear together.）。由於每個語言都有它們習慣組合字詞的方式，所以熟稔搭配詞對於幫助我們正確且道地地使用語言，會有極大的幫助。

例如，我們中文可以說「學習新知」，但是「learn new knowledge」卻是錯誤的英文（正確的應該是「gain / acquire knowledge」）。又例如，當要表達「確切的日期」時，母語人士會直覺地想起「a firm date」，這也是搭配詞的功勞。而母語人士像「公式」（formulaic expression）般地使用出「stand a stark contrast to」（和～大相徑庭），同樣是搭配詞互相結合的產物。

英文母語人士在習得搭配詞時是一個較自然、不費力的過程甚至有可能不自覺，但對於成人第二外語學習者來說，由於先天、後天條件和學習環境都較不利，需要有一個管道，才能接觸到眾多的搭配詞。

因為這樣的一個契機，我從 2015 年起辦了超過 200 場英文搭配詞免費公開課，同時也出版了《搭配詞的力量 Collocations：名詞篇》、《搭配詞的力量 Collocations：形容詞篇》二書。這次動詞篇的出版，期望能讓眾多語言學習愛好者的英文更上一層樓。本書集結了眾搭配詞字典（Macmillan Collocations Dictionary, Oxford Collocations Dictionary, BBI Combinatory Dictionary of English, Longman Collocations Dictionary and Thesaurus）和眾

多語料庫，整理出來臺灣人最需要的搭配詞。因目前市面上的搭配詞用書，大多是厚重的字典，沒有中文翻譯輔助，有時也過度繁雜，比較像是工具書，其實不太適合學習者直接學習。

　　最後，期盼《搭配詞的力量》一系列三本書站在巨人的肩膀上，能夠提供給對學習搭配詞有興趣的臺灣學習者最直接的幫助。希望本書能成為學習者一個新的立基點，有效提升英文能力，不再「字字是英文，句句不是英文」、「年年學英文，年年從頭學」。

創勝文教共同創辦人

王梓沅

2022 年 7 月

搭配詞如何給你力量？
為何搭配詞那麼重要呢？

> 到底什麼是「搭配詞」（collocations）呢？
> 定義上來看，搭配詞就是每個語言約定俗成上的字詞搭配方式。
> 而那些特別高頻的搭配詞組，即泛稱為搭配詞。

搭配詞如何給你力量？為何搭配詞那麼重要呢？

★你是否有想要講一句話，但是語塞講不出來，因為「不知道要用什麼字表達心中所想的東西」的經驗呢？

★你是否有時會覺得自己的英文看似「字字是英文」，但其實「句句不是英文」，不知如何道地、精準地使用英文呢？

★你是否知道的單字不少，但是真的用出來的總是那些呢？

　　如果你曾經有以上的感覺過，那麼很可能代表你的英文搭配詞記得不夠多喔！母語人士之所以講話能如此精準、流利，其中一個原因來自於他們頭腦中有眾多的搭配詞，幫助他們有效率、精準地表達想法。若我們用中文習慣的方式去思考字與字的組合，就很容易造成很多的「台式英文」（Chinglish），我們直接來看看以下幾個字組。

　　對中文為母語的人士來說，我們會不假思索地講出「吃藥」。但對英美人士來講，「eat medicine」卻是個錯誤的表達方式（英文：take medicine）。而你知道嗎，在日文裡頭，他們的藥是用喝的喔（日文：藥を飲む）！

這樣的差異，其實在語言中，屢見不鮮。例如，我們再來看看中文、英文在祝賀人生日時的差異。

對於中文為母語的人士來説，「生日快樂」是我們會不假思索使用的。但你有注意到嗎？對我們的「中文耳」而言，「Happy Birthday」（生日開心）這樣的賀詞，是較不通順的。但「Happy」這個字，「開心」跟「快樂」都是合理的翻譯時，我們的「中文腦」要如何去做選擇呢？而日本人卻是用「お誕生日おめでとうございます。」（生日恭喜）呢！

《搭配詞的力量 Collocations：動詞篇》一書，即因應臺灣人學習英文的需求而生。我從語料庫中整理出英文學習者頻繁使用的動詞，並列出和其搭配使用的名詞以及慣用法等，並精選例句輔以學習，希望能夠加深大家對這些高頻動詞的認識。

例如，中文我們説「漲價」、「引起質疑」、「提高標準」、「發問」的「漲、引起、提高、發」，在翻譯成英文使用時，竟然全部都可以用「raise」來表達（raise prices / raise doubts / raise standards / raise questions）。若我們從小就有搭配詞的意識，想想看我們一路的英文學習會順利多少呢？

一個語言要學好，一定要用對方法。希望這本書所載錄的搭配詞，能帶給大家在學習英文上，滿滿的力量。

Happy learning.

範例：Achieve

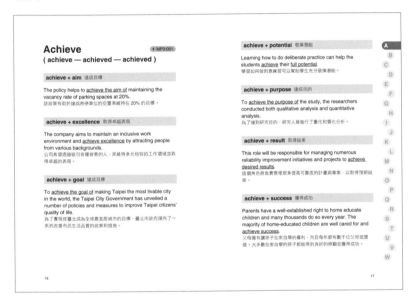

創勝文教共同創辦人

王梓沅

2022 年 7 月

目次

序 002

搭配詞如何給你力量 005

A	**016**
Achieve	016
Acquire	018
Adopt	020
Attain	022

B	**024**
Bear	024
Beat	027
Bend	030
Bolster	032
Boost	034
Break	037

C	**041**
Carry	041
Cast	044
Catch	047
Commit	050
Contract	052
Cut	053

D | 057

Deepen	057
Deliver	059
Develop	061
Dismiss	063
Dispel	066
Disturb	068
Draw	070
Drop	073
Others	076

E | 078

Eliminate	078
Embrace	081
Exercise	083
Exert	086
Expand	088
Evade	091
Others	093

F | 095

Facilitate	095
Field	098
File	100
Fill	102
Fix	105
Follow	108

Formulate	111
Foster	114
Others	117

G   118

Gain	118
Garner	123
Gather	124
Generate	125
Grab	127
Grasp	130

H   133

Harm	133
Hinder	135
Hit	138
Hold	143

I   147

Illustrate	147
Implement	148
Impede	151
Impose	154
Improve	156
Increase	158
Induce	162
Influence	163

Interrupt   165

Invade   166

Irritate   168

J   169

Jeopardize   169

Justify   171

K   174

Kick   174

Knock   175

L   177

Lay   177

Lead   180

Leave   183

Lift   186

Lighten   189

Lodge   191

Lower   192

M   194

Maintain   194

Make   196

Meet   201

Minimize   204

Mitigate 207

Move 209

N 211

Navigate 211

Neglect 212

Nourish 214

Nurture 216

O 218

Obey 218

Offer 220

Omit 224

Organize 226

Outline 229

Overcome 232

Oversee 235

Overthrow 237

P 238

Perform 238

Place 242

Pose 245

Possess 247

Preserve 249

Produce 251

Prohibit 253

Pull	255
Pursue	257
Push	260
Put	262

Q	**266**
Quash	266
Quell	267
Quench	269

R	**270**
Raise	270
Ratify	275
Reach	276
Realize	279
Reap	281
Rebuild	282
Recap	284
Reconcile	285
Rectify	286
Reduce	287
Refine	292
Relax	293
Release	295
Relieve	297
Repair	300
Repel	302

Resolve	303
Retain	306
Reveal	307
Revise	309
Revitalize	311
Ruin	312
Run	314

S   318

Scratch	318
Seal	320
Settle	322
Snatch	325
Soothe	327
Spare	329
Spark	330
Stir	332
Strengthen	333
Stretch	335

T   337

Tackle	337
Take	339
Tell	343
Terminate	345
Throw	346
Thwart	348

Tighten   349

U   351

Uncover   351
Undermine   353
Underscore   355
Unlock   356
Unpack   357
Unravel   358
Unveil   359
Uphold   361
Upset   362
Utilize   364

V   366

Vaccinate   366
Vary   367
Violate   368
Voice   370

W   371

Waive   371
Walk   372
Wane   373
Withdraw   375

Achieve

▶ MP3-001

(achieve — achieved — achieved)

achieve + aim 達成目標

The policy helps to <u>achieve the aim of</u> maintaining the vacancy rate of parking spaces at 20%.

該政策有助於達成將停車位的空置率維持在 20% 的目標。

achieve + excellence 取得卓越表現

The company aims to maintain an inclusive work environment and <u>achieve excellence</u> by attracting people from various backgrounds.

公司希望透過吸引各種背景的人，來維持多元包容的工作環境並取得卓越的表現。

achieve + goal 達成目標

To <u>achieve the goal of</u> making Taipei the most livable city in the world, the Taipei City Government has unveiled a number of policies and measures to improve Taipei citizens' quality of life.

為了實現使臺北成為全球最宜居城市的目標，臺北市政府頒布了一系列改善市民生活品質的政策和措施。

achieve + potential 發揮潛能

Learning how to do deliberate practice can help the students <u>achieve</u> their <u>full potential</u>.
學習如何做刻意練習可以幫助學生充分發揮潛能。

achieve + purpose 達成目的

To <u>achieve the purpose of</u> the study, the researchers conducted both qualitative analysis and quantitative analysis.
為了達到研究目的，研究人員進行了量化和質化分析。

achieve + result 取得結果

This role will be responsible for managing numerous reliability improvement initiatives and projects to <u>achieve desired results</u>.
這個角色將負責管理眾多提高可靠度的計畫與專案，以取得預期結果。

achieve + success 獲得成功

Parents have a well-established right to home educate children and many thousands do so every year. The majority of home-educated children are well cared for and <u>achieve success</u>.
父母擁有讓孩子在家自學的權利，而且每年都有數千位父母這麼做。大多數在家自學的孩子都能得到良好的照顧並獲得成功。

Acquire

▶ MP3-002

(acquire — acquired — acquired)

acquire + asset 收購資產

The leading telecom operator intends to promote growth by <u>acquiring</u> its competitor's <u>assets</u> instead of buying stock.
這家龍頭電信商打算透過收購競爭對手的資產,而不是購買股票,來追求公司成長。

acquire + habit 養成習慣

Most researchers agree that there isn't enough evidence about the benefits of coffee to encourage non-coffee drinkers to <u>acquire the habit</u>.
多數研究人員都認為,目前還沒有足夠證據證明咖啡的好處,無法去鼓勵不喝咖啡的人養成喝咖啡的習慣。

acquire + knowledge 學習、獲得知識

Technology is critical to learning and teaching in the 21st century. There will have to be a revolution in teaching methods to better help students <u>acquire knowledge</u>.
科技對於 21 世紀的教與學至關重要。為了更加幫助學生學習知識,教學方法必須大大改變。

acquire + language　學習語言

Most children <u>acquire language</u> almost automatically at a very young age.
多數孩子在很小的時候幾乎就自然而然學會語言。

acquire + reputation　獲得名聲

These exhibitions helped him <u>acquire a national reputation</u>, and he was invited to become one of the founding members of the Royal Academy in 1769.
這些展覽讓他享譽全國，並於 1769 年受邀成為皇家藝術學院的創始成員之一。

acquire + skill　學習技能

Marketing is the hardest <u>skill</u> to <u>acquire</u> for most new business owners.
對於大多數的新企業主來說，行銷是最難掌握的技能。

Adopt

(adopt — adopted — adopted)

adopt + approach 採取方式

Since our research so far has not produced any solutions to this problem, we need to <u>adopt a different approach to</u> it.
我們的研究到目前為止尚未找出這個問題的答案,因此我們需要採取其他方法。

adopt + child 領養小孩

The couple, who had struggled to get pregnant, decided to <u>adopt a child</u>.
這對一直努力想要懷孕的夫妻決定領養一個孩子。

adopt + lifestyle 採用～生活方式

The information motivates people to <u>adopt a healthy lifestyle</u>, which can reduce cancer risk.
這些資訊促使人們用健康的方式過生活,進而降低罹癌的風險。

adopt + method 採用方法

The organization said most countries could <u>adopt the method</u> at little additional cost to existing treatment strategies.
該組織表示,多數國家都可以採用這個方法,而不太需要增加現有治療策略的成本。

adopt + policy 採用政策

It was a most fruitful discussion, with both sides agreeing to <u>adopt a common policy</u>.
這是最有成效的一次討論，雙方都同意採用共同的政策。

adopt + standard 採用標準

Companies will now have the option to <u>adopt the standard</u> for their next set of accounts. The rule will, however, become mandatory by 2024.
公司現在可以選擇要不要在他們的下一套帳戶採用這個標準。不過，到 2024 年，該規定將成為強制性規定。

adopt + strategy 採取策略

To date, policymakers have been most reluctant to <u>adopt</u> either of the <u>strategies</u>.
到目前為止，政策制定者最不願意採取這兩種策略。

Attain

▶ MP3-004

(attain — attained — attained)

attain + age 達到年齡

There are a disproportionate number of younger voters, many of whom might neglect to enroll when they <u>attain the voting age</u>.

年輕選民的數量特別多，其中許多人在達到投票年齡時可能會忘了登記。

attain + fame 獲得名聲

He was one of the first black American artists to <u>attain</u> such a level of <u>fame</u> and success.

他是前幾位獲得如此聲望和成功的美國黑人藝術家之一。

attain + goal 達到目標

Our brains focus on the task in hand to <u>attain a goal</u>. Once we perceive that our goal is complete, we shift attention elsewhere.

我們的大腦會專注在手上的任務以達成目標。一旦我們意識到目標已經完成，我們就會將注意力轉移到其他地方。

attain + happiness 得到快樂、幸福

All you need to do is expand ever increasing amounts of effort to <u>attain happiness</u>.

你需要做的就是付出更多努力來得到幸福。

attain + mastery 達到精通

Most people find such mathematical <u>mastery</u> either impossible to <u>attain</u>, or attained only at the expense of an enormous amount of highly unpleasant work.

大多數人發現要對數學達到精通是不可能的，或者是需要付出非常大的功夫，而且是很辛苦、不舒服的過程。

attain + objective 達到目標

The government is now on track to <u>attain the objective of</u> zero deaths from malaria by 2021.

政府現在有望在 2021 年之前實現瘧疾零死亡的目標。

attain + success 獲得成功

People who <u>attain success</u> have learned to forget past failures and concentrate on present goals.

成功的人都學著忘記過去的失敗，專注在眼前的目標。

Bear

▶ MP3-005

(bear — bore — born)

bear + arms 攜帶武器

After the school shooting, the question about whether people should have the right to keep and <u>bear arms</u> came to the fore.
在發生校園槍擊事件之後，人們是否有權持有和攜帶槍枝的問題浮出檯面。

bear + brunt 承受影響、衝擊

Agricultural workers continue to <u>bear the brunt of</u> difficult conditions and extreme weather.
農人繼續首當其衝承受艱困工作環境和極端氣候的影響。

bear + burden 承受負擔

People who will mainly <u>bear the burden of</u> the tax are workers earning lower wages.
主要承受這個稅收負擔的是工資較低的人。

bear + fruit 獲得成果

Mr. Joseph admits that tax and education reform, though essential, will take many years to <u>bear fruit</u>.
Joseph 坦承，稅收和教育改革雖然相當重要，但要花很多年的時間才能得到成果。

bear + resemblance 具有相似性

The new car <u>bears a strong resemblance to</u> other C-Class models, especially around the nose.
這款新車與其他 C-Class 車款非常相似，尤其是在車頭的部分。

bear + responsibility 承擔責任

The side that wins custody is assumed to <u>bear all responsibility for</u> raising the child.
得到監護權的一方，被認為要負起撫養孩子的所有責任。

bear + suspense 耐著性子

Grandmother always brings gifts and the kids cannot <u>bear the suspense of</u> wondering what she may be bringing this time.
奶奶總是帶禮物來，而孩子們會耐不住性子開始猜她這次會帶什麼。

bear + witness 見證

Reporters will continue to <u>bear witness to</u> the historic events that are taking place in Hong Kong.
記者將繼續見證香港正在發生的歷史性事件。

實用短語 / 用法 / 句型

1. bear in mind that... 記得～、把～謹記在心

Please <u>bear in mind that</u> this train will terminate at the Daan Station rather than the Xiangshan Station.

請記得，本列車的終點站為大安站，而不是象山站。

Beat

▶ MP3-006

(beat — beat — beaten)

beat + egg 把蛋打勻

Then, in a mixing bowl, gently <u>beat</u> the <u>eggs</u> together with a pinch of salt and pepper.
然後，在攪拌碗中，加入少許的鹽和胡椒，和蛋一起輕輕攪拌打勻。

beat + record 打破紀錄

If the game continues, chances are high that he could <u>beat the record</u> set by Kobe Bryant.
如果比賽繼續進行，他很有可能會打破 Kobe Bryant 的紀錄。

beat + rush 避開尖峰時段

Hundreds of travelers headed out of town Wednesday evening, hoping to <u>beat the</u> Chinese New Year's <u>rush</u>.
數百名旅客在週三晚上離開市區，希望能避開春節的尖峰時段。

beat + system 打破系統、制度的限制

Although regulations limit the data transfer rate, the man did what he could to <u>beat the system</u>.
儘管法規限制了數據傳輸速率，但他還是竭盡所能打破系統的限制。

beat + traffic 避開交通壅塞

Most companies at the Nangang Software Park tend to allow employees to head home earlier on Fridays to <u>beat the traffic</u>.

大多數南港軟體園區的公司都傾向讓員工在週五早點回家，以避開交通壅塞。

實用短語 / 用法 / 句型

1. beat a path to one's door 搶著要得到某人

If you do something very well, and focus on that, people will <u>beat a path to your door</u>.

如果你把一件事做得很好，並且持續專注在這件事上，人們就會搶著要你。

2. beat around the bush （說話）拐彎抹角

Most candidates <u>beat around the bush</u> on controversial topics like healthcare and taxes.

大多數候選人在醫療保健和稅收等爭議性議題上都拐彎抹角。

3. beat one's head against the wall 白費力氣、徒勞無功

Some people are never going to agree with you on this policy, so it's no use <u>beating your head against the wall</u> trying to convince everyone.

在這個政策上，有些人永遠不會同意你的意見，所以你拚命想要說服所有人是沒有用的。

4. beat one's brains out 絞盡腦汁、用盡全力

Our marketing team <u>beat their brains out</u> trying to come up with a solution.

我們的行銷團隊用盡全力試圖找出解決方案。

5. beat the drum 支持、宣傳

At first the legalization of same-sex marriage didn't seem to have much support, but recently I've seen more people <u>beating the drum</u> online.

起初，同性婚姻的合法化似乎沒有得到很多支持，但最近我看到越來越多人在網路上發聲支持。

Bend

▶ MP3-007

(bend — bent — bent)

bend + law　鑽法律漏洞

Through lobbying, corporations get out of paying their fair share of taxes, <u>bend the law</u> to protect their interests and pass the costs on to consumers.

透過遊說，企業規避了應繳的稅款、鑽法律漏洞保護自己的利益，並將成本轉嫁給消費者。

bend + rules　變通、通融、放寬規定

Can't you <u>bend the rules</u> a little and let me in? I was only a few minutes late.

你就不能稍微通融一下讓我進去嗎？我只是遲到幾分鐘而已。

bend + truth　扭曲事實

As with most political debates, both sides only present the facts that support their arguments, and in some cases <u>bend the truth</u>.

就像大部分的政治辯論一樣，雙方只提出支持他們論點的事實，而在某些情況下扭曲事實。

實用短語 / 用法 / 句型

1. bend one's ear 對某人一直講（使人覺得不耐煩）

Stanley has been <u>bending my ear about</u> the stock market for the past hour!

Stanley 一直跟我講股市的事，講了一個小時了！

2. bend one's efforts 專心致力、全力投入

I've been <u>bending my efforts to</u> find a way out of these legal problems, but, as of now, I'm still in trouble.

我一直努力找方法解決這些法律問題，但到目前為止，我還是沒解決。

3. bend one's / the elbow 喝酒（特別指喝太多、喝醉）

If he is so hungover, he must have <u>bent the elbow</u> at the party last night.

如果他還在宿醉，他昨晚的聚會肯定喝超多。

4. bend one's mind 專心致力、全力投入

The psychologist makes it her mission to <u>bend her mind to</u> scientific insights that help kids thrive.

這位心理學家把投入可以幫助孩童發展的科學觀察視為是自己的使命。

Bolster

▶ MP3-008

(bolster — bolstered — bolstered)

bolster + argument 支持論點

The results of the study <u>bolster the argument</u> that some consumers do not respond to economic incentives.
這項研究的結果證明，有些消費者對經濟誘因沒有反應。

bolster + confidence 提升信心

A third success will <u>bolster confidence in</u> the country's space program, which has suffered a series of setbacks in recent years.
第三次成功將提升對該國太空計畫的信心，這計畫近年來歷經了一番波折。

bolster + claim 支持說法

The documents filed late Wednesday <u>bolster that claim</u> and also describe an effort by the health minister to keep the face mask market stable.
週三晚上發的資料支持了那個說法，並說明了衛生部長為了穩定口罩市場所做的努力。

bolster + economy 振興經濟

President Obama sent Congress a jobs bill, aiming to put over a million Americans back to work and help <u>bolster the economy</u> against outside shocks.

總統 Obama 向國會提交了一項就業法案，旨在使超過 100 萬的美國人重返工作崗位，並幫助振興經濟、抵抗外部衝擊。

bolster + image 改善、提升形象

The Communist Party, keen to <u>bolster its image</u> at home, wants the international event to appear successful.

迫切想提升國內形象的中國共產黨希望此次國際活動可以成功。

bolster + morale 提升、鼓舞士氣

The boss gave the team a pep talk to <u>bolster morale</u> during these trying times.

在這艱困的時局，老闆向團隊講了一番激勵性的談話來提升士氣。

bolster + spirits 提振心情

Mayor Michael Bloomberg defended the use of public resources as a way to <u>bolster the</u> economy and <u>spirits of</u> New Yorkers.

市長 Michael Bloomberg 為公共資源的使用做辯護，說明這是振興經濟和提振紐約人精神的方法。

Boost

▶ MP3-009

(boost — boosted — boosted)

boost + competitiveness 提升競爭力

The South Korean president aims to privatize state-run
companies to <u>boost competitiveness</u>.
南韓總統計劃將國有企業私有化，以提高競爭力。

boost + confidence 提升信心

Those policies have helped <u>boost confidence among</u>
consumers, making them feel wealthier and more willing to
spend.
這些政策有助於提升消費者的信心，使他們感到更富裕、更願意消
費。

boost + economy 振興經濟

Reserve President Richard Fisher said the Fed is facing
financial storms. He suggested fiscal and regulatory
changes were needed to help <u>boost the economy</u>.
達拉斯聯邦準備銀行總裁 Richard Fisher 說，聯準會正面臨金融風
暴。他表示需要進行財政和監管方面的改革，以促進經濟成長。

boost + morale 提升、鼓舞士氣

When the staff worked around the clock to meet deadlines, the manager sometimes brought coffee in to <u>boost morale</u>.
當員工日以繼夜趕在截止日前完工，經理有時會帶咖啡給大家以鼓舞士氣。

boost + number 提高數字

The Tokyo 2020 Olympics were expected to help <u>boost the number of</u> visitors to Japan.
預計 2020 年東京奧運將有助於增加日本的遊客人數。

boost + performance 提升表現

Workplace studies show recognition and appreciation <u>boost performance</u> better than criticism.
職場研究顯示，認可和讚賞比批評更能提高工作表現。

boost + productivity 提高生產力

Some companies aim to <u>boost productivity</u> by investing in their employees' general happiness.
有些公司打算透過投資員工的整體幸福感來提高生產力。

boost + revenue 提高收益

The advertising company is fighting back with a host of measures to cut costs and <u>boost revenue</u>.
這家廣告公司正採取一系列的手段進行反擊，以削減成本、提高收益。

boost + sales 提高銷售量、刺激銷售

The successful branding and marketing of the new beer has already <u>boosted sales</u> and increased profits.
這款新啤酒的品牌推廣和行銷活動的成功已經提高了銷量和利潤。

boost + tourism 振興觀光、促進旅遊

Recognizing that the financial industry may not feed the cities forever, mayors in both places hope to <u>boost tourism</u>.
認知到金融產業可能無法一直供養著城市，兩地市長都希望能促進觀光。

Break

▶ MP3-010

(break — broke — broken)

break + deadlock 打破僵局

Somebody will have to compromise if we are to <u>break the deadlock</u> between the two warring factions.
如果我們要打破雙方交戰的僵局，就必須要有人妥協。

break + habit 改掉習慣

About 90 percent of cigarette smokers in the United States tried to <u>break the habit</u>, but most of them failed.
美國約有 90% 的吸菸者試著戒菸，但大多數人都失敗了。

break + heart 使～傷心、心碎

Don't date anyone who you think might <u>break your heart</u>.
不要和你認為會讓你心碎的人交往。

break + law 違法、違規

The immigrants did <u>break the law</u>, but to achieve a better life for themselves and their families, not to hurt others.
這些移民確實觸犯了法律，但他們是為了讓自己和家人過上更好的生活，而不是要傷害別人。

break + promise 違背承諾、食言

The political issue has diverted attention from a big tax increase that <u>broke a promise</u> he made in the 2004 election.
這個政治問題轉移了人們對他大幅增稅的注意力，這次的增稅違背了他在 2004 年選舉時所做的承諾。

break + record 打破紀錄

Kobe Bryant's mental toughness, more than his physical abilities, was what allowed him to <u>break the record</u>.
相較於身體素質，Kobe Bryant 強大的心理素質更是他能打破紀錄的關鍵。

break + rule 違反規定

If they <u>break the rule</u> again, the phones will be turned over to their parents and the students will receive a two-hour detention.
如果學生們再次違反規定，手機就會交給父母，並且要被留校察看 2 個小時。

break + silence 打破沉默

It's not clear whether she will <u>break her silence on</u> the allegations against her husband.
關於對她丈夫的指控，目前還不清楚她是否會打破沉默。

break + story 搶先報導

Our newspaper <u>broke the story of</u> the mayor's scandal, and now every national news outlet is covering it!
我們的報紙搶先報導了市長的醜聞，現在全國新聞媒體都在報導這件事！

break + word 違背承諾、食言

Most people think they are liars who will say anything to be re-elected, but <u>break their word</u> once they are in power.
大多數的人都認為他們是騙子，為了連任什麼話都可以說，但一旦掌權就違背承諾。

實用短語 / 用法 / 句型

1. break a leg 祝你好運

Jason sent Phillip a text before Monday's show, with the greeting: "<u>Break a leg</u> and enjoy yourself."
在週一的表演開始前，Jason 傳了訊息給 Phillip：「演出順利，盡情享受表演。」

2. break ground 動土、動工

The president of the company came to <u>break ground on</u> the new corporate headquarters today, but it will be years before we can actually move into it.
今天總裁為新的公司總部動土，但我們還要等好幾年才能真的搬進去。

3. break the bank 使人破產

I don't have enough money to go on a vacation right now; I'm afraid it would <u>break the bank</u>.

我現在沒有足夠的錢去度假，我擔心這會讓我破產。

4. break the ice 破冰、打破沉默

I was so nervous about meeting Samantha's parents for the first time, but her dad immediately <u>broke the ice</u> by asking about my interests, and everything went great after that.

我第一次見到 Samantha 父母時很緊張，但他爸爸立刻問起我的興趣，打破了沉默，從那之後一切都很順利。

Carry

▶ MP3-011

(carry — carried — carried)

carry + blame 承擔責任

If the virus leads to an economic collapse, the province's politicians will have to <u>carry</u> much of <u>the blame</u>.
如果病毒導致經濟崩潰，該州的政治人物將要負起大部分的責任。

carry + burden 承擔責任、背負重擔

These small and medium-sized companies continue to <u>carry the burden of</u> tremendous unemployment or underemployment in the countryside.
這些中小企業持續承擔著鄉下地區大量失業或就業不足的重任。

carry + conviction 具有說服力

Her explanation for stealing money failed to <u>carry conviction</u> in the face of the facts.
事實擺在眼前，她對於偷錢的解釋無法讓人相信。

carry + guarantee 保證、擔保

Many of the offers made to students are unsubsidized loans, which only <u>carry</u> government <u>guarantee</u> but no interest rate subsidy.
許多提供給學生的貸款都是無補貼貸款，這種只有政府做擔保，但沒有利率補貼。

carry + guilt 背負愧疚、罪惡感

As parents, we <u>carry a huge amount of guilt</u> every second of every day for not being with our children.
身為父母，不能陪在孩子身邊，我們每分每秒都深感愧疚。

carry + risk 具有風險

All of these methods have drawbacks and <u>carry environmental risks</u>, as the new study explains.
正如新的研究解釋，這些方法都有缺點並具有對環境造成危害的風險。

carry + weight 具有影響力

Nowadays, influencers share their values on social media, <u>carrying weight in</u> particular subjects.
現在，網紅在社群媒體上分享自己的價值觀，在特定話題上具有影響力。

實用短語 / 用法 / 句型

1. carry a tune 把音唱準

Being able to <u>carry a tune</u> does not automatically equip you to play a role in a musical. You actually need to sound really good, too.
能把音唱準不代表你就有能力擔任音樂劇的一角，你還必須要唱得夠好聽。

2. carry a torch for sb 單戀、暗戀某人

Terry has been <u>carrying a torch for</u> Liz for years, but she isn't aware of that.

Terry 多年來一直暗戀著 Liz，不過 Liz 不知情。

3. carry the day 獲得勝利

The presidential candidate was counting on capturing women's votes to <u>carry the day</u>.

這位總統候選人指望贏得婦女的選票來打贏選戰。

Cast
(cast — cast — cast)

▶ MP3-012

cast + aspersions 詆毀、中傷

Joe has repeatedly tried to <u>cast aspersions on</u> my husband's work and character over the past 30 years.
過去 30 年來，Joe 一直試圖詆毀我老公的工作和性格。

cast + ballot 投票

Three presidential candidates <u>cast their ballots in</u> the presidential and legislative elections on Saturday.
三名總統候選人在週六的總統及立法委員選舉中投下選票。

cast + doubt 對～產生懷疑、質疑

Several studies in recent years have <u>cast doubt on</u> the effectiveness of these laws.
近年來的一些研究使人們質疑這些法律的效力。

cast + light 闡明、解釋

Some studies have attempted to <u>cast light on</u> the outbreak of the novel coronavirus.
有些研究試圖解釋新型冠狀病毒的疫情。

cast + shadow 蒙上陰影

The outbreak of the disease has <u>cast a shadow over</u> European economies and stock markets.
疾病的爆發讓歐洲經濟和股市蒙上了陰影。

cast + spell 施展魔法；使～著迷

The award-winning blockbuster is back, and once again ready to <u>cast its spell on</u> audiences.
這部獲獎大片又回來了，準備再次使觀眾著迷。

cast + suspicion 對～產生懷疑、質疑

The filmmakers thought that this history might muddy the waters and <u>cast suspicion on</u> the motivation of the character, and thus they decided to ignore it.
電影製作人認為，這段歷史可能會造成混淆，讓人懷疑這個角色的動機，因此他們決定忽略它。

cast + vote 投票

In a democracy, people <u>cast their votes</u> to voice their opinions and express their feelings.
在民主國家中，人民投票來表達自己的意見和感受。

實用短語 / 用法 / 句型

1. cast one's mind back 回想

As he <u>cast his mind back to</u> last month, he realized he couldn't think of a single day he'd gone without alcohol.

回想起上個月,他發現自己沒有一天不喝酒。

Catch
(catch — caught — caught)

▶ MP3-013

---

catch + attention 引起注意

Elon Musk is hoping to <u>catch the attention of</u> battery makers or investors to give his idea a try.
Elon Musk 希望引起電池製造商或投資者的注意，來試試看他的想法。

---

catch + cold 感冒；連帶受到影響

It used to be that when the US economy sneezed, the rest of the world <u>caught a cold</u>.
過去的情況是，當美國經濟打個噴嚏，世界其他地區也會連帶受到影響。

---

catch + eye 引起注意、吸引目光

African fashion design has <u>caught the eye of</u> international celebrities including former US first lady Michelle Obama, Rihanna, and Beyoncé.
非洲時裝設計吸引了國際名人的目光，包括了前美國第一夫人 Michelle Obama、Rihanna 和 Beyoncé。

catch + fire 起火

He was sure of winning the race, but as fate would have it, he got stuck in the middle with his car <u>catching fire</u> from nowhere.

他確信自己能贏得這場比賽，但像是命中註定，他被困在半路，而車子不知道從哪裡開始起火。

catch + glimpse 瞥見、看見

The crowd that wished to <u>catch a glimpse of</u> Hugh Jackman seemed to be mainly teenagers.

想看 Hugh Jackman 一眼的人似乎主要都是年輕人。

catch + imagination 引發想像

It would be ethically unacceptable to use techniques to create a human clone. That, however, was the very thing that <u>caught the world's imagination</u>.

利用技術來製造複製人在道德上是不可接受的。然而，這正是引起全世界想像的事情。

catch + interest 引起興趣

The company's technology has <u>caught the interest of</u> a number of companies, including Accenture and Microsoft.

該公司的技術引起了埃森哲和微軟等多家公司的興趣。

catch + ride 搭便車

I was able to <u>catch a ride with</u> a friend who had parked his car at a nearby parking lot to beat the traffic.
我搭朋友的便車，他把車停在附近的停車場以避開車潮。

catch + sight 瞥見、看見

Wendy only <u>caught sight of</u> the burglar for a second, so she couldn't describe his appearance to the police.
Wendy 只瞥到竊賊一秒鐘的時間，所以她無法向員警描述他的外貌。

實用短語 / 用法 / 句型

1. catch sb off guard 使人措手不及

The CEO <u>caught him off guard</u> when she suddenly asked him to introduce himself.
執行長突然要他做自我介紹，讓他措手不及。

2. get caught up in sth （不情願地）被捲入～

They were having an argument and somehow I <u>got caught up in</u> it
他們在吵架，而我莫名其妙地也被捲進去。

3. catch sb red-handed 當場逮到某人

Driving under the influence, he <u>was caught red-handed</u> by the police.
他酒後駕車，被警察當場逮捕。

Commit

(commit — committed — committed)

commit + crime 犯罪

He spent 30 years in prison for <u>a crime</u> that he almost certainly did not <u>commit</u>.
他因為一項幾乎可以肯定沒有犯過的罪行，在監獄裡待了 30 年。

commit + fraud 詐欺

Cloud storage allows users to access music, documents and other files from any mobile device. But cloud services can also be used to launch attacks, send spam and <u>commit fraud</u>.
雲端儲存讓用戶可以從任何行動裝置存取音樂、文件和其他檔案。但是，雲服端務也可以用於發起攻擊、發送垃圾郵件和詐騙。

commit + murder 謀殺

Fresh evidence has recently come to light. It suggests that he didn't in fact <u>commit the murder</u>.
最近新發現的證據顯示，實際上他並沒有殺人。

commit + suicide 自殺

The pesticide is known to be so deadly that some people drink it to <u>commit suicide</u>.
大家都知道這種農藥的致命性很高，以至於有些人喝它自殺。

實用短語 / 用法 / 句型

1. commit sth to memory 牢記～

Students learning Mandarin are expected to <u>commit to memory</u> the sounds of a character at the time it is taught.

學中文的學生應該在學一個字時，就記住它的讀音。

Contract

▶ MP3-015

(contract — contracted — contracted)

contract + disease 染病

Public health experts have warned that children, or anyone with a weakened immune system, can <u>contract the disease</u>.
公共衛生專家警告，兒童或免疫系統較弱的人都可能感染這種疾病。

contract + virus 感染病毒

Wearing a mask will not prevent you from <u>contracting the virus</u>, but it surely will reduce the risk.
戴口罩無法使你免於感染病毒，但它肯定可以降低感染的機率。

contract + flu 感染流感

People may <u>contract flu</u> by touching something with viruses on it and then touching their mouth or nose.
人們可能會因為接觸帶有病毒的東西，然後觸摸口鼻而感染流感。

contract + pneumonia 感染肺炎

Millions of people in the US <u>contract pneumonia</u> annually and, like other infectious diseases, it can be life-threatening.
在美國，每年有數百萬人感染肺炎，它和其他傳染性疾病一樣都可能危及性命。

Cut

(cut — cut — cut)

cut + costs 降低成本

With the economy ailing, companies are seeking to <u>cut costs</u> by slashing retirement benefits.
由於經濟不景氣，各公司都在尋求透過大幅刪減退休福利來降低成本。

cut + deal 達成協議、達成交易

The carmaker has <u>cut a deal with</u> unions to limit pay raises.
該汽車製造商與工會達成了一項限制加薪的協議。

cut + jobs 裁員

Spending may continue to decline as companies reduce employees' hours or <u>cut jobs</u>.
隨著公司減少員工的工時或裁員，支出可能會繼續降低。

cut + prices 降低價格

Prices fell as energy costs dropped and merchants <u>cut prices on</u> cars and clothes.
隨著能源成本下降，商家降低了汽車和服裝的價格。

cut + rates 降低利率

Some economists believe that the government will <u>cut interest rates</u> again before the spring. But it no longer has much room to <u>cut rates</u> further if the economy takes a deep dive.

一些經濟學家認為，政府將在春季前再次降息。但如果經濟大幅下滑，不會再有進一步降息的空間。

cut + spending 減少開銷

The administration and the opposition agree on the need to <u>cut spending</u>, but differ on the details.

政府和在野黨都同意有必要減少開銷，但在細節上有所分歧。

cut + taxes 減稅

The lawmaker vowed to <u>cut taxes</u>, rein in powerful trades unions and reduce public spending.

這位國會議員誓言要減稅、控制強大的工會、並減少公共支出。

實用短語 / 用法 / 句型

1. cut both ways 有好也有壞、是把雙面刃

Casting a couple of big movie stars in a Broadway play can <u>cut both ways</u>—audiences may stand in line for tickets, but critics can put on their scowling "show-me" faces.

找來大咖影星出演百老匯音樂劇有利有弊：觀眾可能會排隊買票，但劇評們可能會擺出一副「等著看」的樣子。

2. cut corners （做事）貪圖方便、便宜；偷工減料

Inflationary pressure encourages even well-intentioned companies to <u>cut corners</u> and make profits.

通貨膨脹壓力甚至會使立意良善的公司偷工減料，以賺取利潤。

3. cut sb short 打斷某人的話

Sorry, but I'm going to have to <u>cut you short</u>, though, since I'm on my way to a party.

抱歉，我得打斷你一下，因為我正要去參加一個聚會。

4. cut sb some slack 對某人網開一面、放過某人一次

It's perfectly understandable that he would make such a mistake. <u>Cut him some slack</u>. He's still new here.

他會犯這樣的錯完全可以理解。放過他一次吧。他還是新來的。

5. cut sb to the quick / bone 傷了某人的心

Anything would have been better than this ice-cold contempt that <u>cut her to the quick</u>.

沒有什麼事比這種無情的鄙視還更傷她的心。

6. cut one's losses 及時撤出、收手以減少損失

Sometimes it is better to <u>cut your losses</u> and move forward, before prices drop even further.

有時在價格跌更多之前，及時收手並繼續往前走是更好的選擇。

7. cut (no) ice with sb 對某人（沒）有影響

That statement <u>cut no ice with</u> voters, who reminded the governor that in one of his election campaigns he had promised legislative pay raises.

那份聲明沒有對選民產生任何影響，選民們提醒州長，在他的一次競選活動中，他曾承諾會透過立法提高工資。

8. cut to the chase 開門見山地說、直接切入重點

I didn't have much time to talk so I <u>cut to the chase</u> and asked whether he was still married.

我沒有太多時間聊天，所以我就開門見山問他是否還和他老婆在一起。

Deepen

(deepen — deepen — deepen)

deepen + understanding 加深理解

This method helps students <u>deepen their understanding of</u> the topic as they connect new ideas and information to prior knowledge.

這種方法有助於學生加深對主題的理解，因為他們將新的想法和資訊，與既有的知識做連結。

deepen + knowledge 加深知識、了解

The couple had talked for some time about moving to an Arab country to learn the language and <u>deepen their knowledge of</u> their religion.

這對夫妻已經討論了一段時間，是否要移居阿拉伯國家學習語言、並加深對宗教的了解。

deepen + relationship 加深關係

When we had the opportunity to put a pitch proposal together to <u>deepen the relationship with</u> the corporation, we knew this could be a game changer for us.

當我們有機會一起提出提案來加深與這間公司的關係時，我們知道這可能是個徹底翻轉的契機。

deepen + faith 加深信念

The Russia-Ukraine war has <u>deepened their faith in</u> democracy.

烏俄戰爭加深了他們對民主的信念。

Deliver

▶ MP3-018

(deliver — delivered — delivered)

deliver + goods 運送貨物、交貨

We shall <u>deliver your goods</u> within a maximum of 30 days beginning with the date of the order. If goods are not available, we will inform you and reimburse any sum already paid within 30 days.

我們將於訂單日起算的 30 天內出貨。如果商品沒有庫存，我們將通知您，並於 30 天內退還所有已經支付的款項。

deliver + services 提供服務

Compared with public sectors, private firms that promise to <u>deliver services</u> at low cost are an attractive option to customers.

與公部門相比，承諾以低價提供服務的私人企業對顧客來説，是一個吸引人的選項。

deliver + message 傳遞訊息

Before a keynote speech, give yourself enough time to practice so you can <u>deliver your message</u> with confidence.

在做專題演講之前，給自己足夠的時間練習，這樣你才能自信地傳遞資訊。

deliver + speech 發表演説

The vice president was invited to <u>deliver the commencement speech</u> at the University of Pennsylvania.
副總統受邀到賓州大學發表畢業演説。

deliver + talk 發表言論

She had a colleague <u>deliver the talk</u> in her place, and added a brief message explaining her absence.
她請一位同事替她報告，並附上一則簡短的訊息解釋為什麼缺席。

deliver + baby 生小孩

Two days before Christmas, she went into labor and <u>delivered a</u> healthy <u>baby</u>.
她在聖誕節前兩天臨盆，生下了一個健康的寶寶。

實用短語 / 用法 / 句型

1. deliver on one's promise 履行承諾

If the government can begin to <u>deliver on its promises</u>, it should help both the currency and the stock market.
如果政府能夠開始履行承諾，對貨幣和股市應該都會有幫助。

Develop

▶ MP3-019

(develop — developed — developed)

develop + skill 培養技能

In this course, we will help you <u>develop</u> all <u>the skills</u> needed to communicate effectively in a corporate setting.
在這門課中，我們會幫助你培養在職場環境中有效溝通所需的所有技能。

develop + strategy 制訂、發展策略

We can't <u>develop strategies</u> to deal with this until we know the scope of the problem.
在了解問題的大小之前，我們無法制訂應對的策略。

develop + framework 擬定框架、體系

We need to <u>develop an analytical framework for</u> the campaign to understand and improve its performance.
我們需要為這次的宣傳活動制定一個分析框架，以了解和改善其成效。

develop + awareness 提高意識

The team plans to <u>develop awareness</u> within the local community <u>of</u> the need to drink purified water.
這個小組計劃在當地提高人們對飲用純淨水的意識。

develop + knowledge 拓展知識

Office workers are now encouraged to use online learning to <u>develop knowledge</u> and skills <u>in</u> their respective areas.
辦公室的職員現在被鼓勵利用線上學習來拓展各自領域的知識與技能。

develop + idea 發展想法

The manager suggested she should engage in creative work and <u>develop new ideas for</u> the business.
經理建議她應該從事創造性的工作，想出新的生意點子。

develop + concept 發想概念

When creative thinkers <u>develop a concept</u>, they've got to convince an investor or a group to sign off on it with funding.
當具有創意的人發想出概念時，他們必須說服投資人或團體拿出資金來投資。

Dismiss

▶ MP3-020

(dismiss — dismissed — dismissed)

dismiss + case　撤銷案件

His lawyer says he would like to <u>get the case dismissed</u> before the old man dies.
他的律師説，他想在老先生過世之前讓案件撤銷。

dismiss + idea　駁斥想法

He <u>dismissed the idea</u> that fertility rates declined as populations grew wealthier.
他駁斥了生育率會隨著人民富裕程度提高而下降的觀點。

dismiss + possibility　駁斥可能性

Last week the spokesman <u>dismissed the possibility</u> that the airline would soon be forced to raise fares to compensate for currency losses.
發言人上週否認了航空公司將快被迫提高票價以補償匯差損失的可能性。

dismiss + charge　駁回指控

The judge <u>dismissed the charge</u> as unfounded, acknowledging the accuser had a history of making false allegations.
法官認為指控毫無根據而駁回，並認定原告有不實指控的紀錄。

dismiss + suggestion 拒絕建議

If coming from anyone else, <u>the suggestion</u> would have <u>been dismissed</u> as ludicrous.
如果是別人提出這個建議，會被認為很荒唐而不被接受。

dismiss + thought 駁斥看法

Howard <u>dismissed the thought</u> that he failed to meet expectations and instead provided his own spin.
Howard 不認為自己沒有符合期望，反倒是提出了自己的觀點。

dismiss + criticism 駁斥批評

He <u>dismissed criticism</u> that he had failed to speak out forcefully enough about the growing unrest in Iran.
他駁斥了有關他沒有替伊朗日益加劇的動盪說話的批評。

dismiss + complaint 駁回申訴

<u>The complaint was dismissed</u> by the commission's staff, and the issue seemed dead.
投訴被委員會的人駁回，這個問題似乎也已經不重要。

dismiss + appeal 駁回上訴

In their judgment, the five supreme court justices unanimously <u>dismissed the appeal</u>.
五名最高法院的法官在判決中都駁回了上訴。

實用短語 / 用法 / 句型

1. dismiss sth out of hand （想都沒想）馬上駁回～

No idea, no matter how seemingly outlandish, should <u>be dismissed out of hand</u>.

無論聽起來多奇怪，任何想法都不應該想都沒想就馬上被拒絕。

Dispel

▶ MP3-021

(dispel — dispelled — dispelled)

dispel + idea 推翻想法

The Fed and other regulators must do something to <u>dispel the idea</u> that financial institutions are too big to fail.
聯準會和其他監管機構必須有些作為，以推翻金融機構大到不能倒的說法。

dispel + myth 打破迷思

The article is to <u>dispel the myth</u> that fast food is cheaper than healthy meals prepared at home.
這篇文章是為了打破速食比在家準備的健康餐還便宜的迷思。

dispel + notion 推翻想法

Our chief purpose is to <u>dispel the notion</u> that nothing can be done.
我們主要的目的是推翻什麼也做不了的想法。

dispel + impression 打破印象

It is hard to <u>dispel the impression</u> that the main thing was only to give the summiteers something new to talk about.
人們很難打破，認為高峰會的主要目的，只是為了讓與會者有新話題可以談論這樣的印象。

dispel + doubts 消除疑慮

If the euro is to survive the debt crisis, Europe's leaders will have to <u>dispel public doubts about</u> its survival.
如果歐元要在歐債危機中存活下來，歐洲領導人必須消除大眾對歐元未來的疑慮。

dispel + mystery 解開謎團

The official statements have done little to <u>dispel the mystery</u>.
官方的聲明並沒有解開這個謎團。

dispel + fear 消除恐懼

Friday's report on the gross domestic product certainly did nothing to <u>dispel the fears</u>.
星期五公布的國內生產毛額（GDP）報告顯然沒能消除這個恐懼。

Disturb

(disturb — disturbed — disturbed)

disturb + peace 擾亂和平

After the walkouts, he was arrested and charged with conspiracy to <u>disturb the peace of</u> the country.
罷工後，他被逮捕並被指控串謀擾亂國家和平。

disturb + sleep 影響睡眠

You might want to avoid drinking coffee and tea before bed because they can <u>disturb your sleep</u>.
你可能要避免在睡前喝咖啡和茶，因為它們會影響你的睡眠。

disturb + rest 打擾休息

When people call or come by and <u>disturb your rest</u>, try to tell them plainly you do not want to be disturbed at a certain time.
當有人來電或來訪打擾到你休息時，試著直接告訴他們，你不想在特定時段被打擾。

disturb + mind 擾亂思緒

I didn't pursue him. I knew that if I did start hanging around with him, he was going to <u>disturb my mind</u>.
我沒有追他。我知道，如果我真的開始和他在一起，他會擾亂我的思緒。

disturb + concentration 影響注意力

I've got to go. I couldn't work with the kids around because they would <u>disturb my concentration</u>.

我得走了。有孩子在旁邊我沒辦法工作，因為他們會影響我的注意力。

disturb + thoughts 干擾思緒

Her <u>thoughts were disturbed</u> again by heavy traffic noise.

她的思緒又被車輛吵雜的聲音擾亂了。

實用短語 / 用法 / 句型

1. sorry to disturb you 抱歉打擾（口語）

<u>Sorry to disturb you</u> at this time of night, but I have an urgent message.

很抱歉這麼晚打擾你，但我有個緊急的消息。

Draw

(draw — drew — drawn)

draw + attention 引起注意

The statistics also <u>draw attention to</u> the changing position of women in society.
這些統計數字也使人們注意到女性社會地位的變化。

draw + conclusion 下結論

It is too early to <u>draw a conclusion</u>, given that the presidential election is still 18 months away.
距離總統大選還有 18 個月，現在下結論還太早。

draw + inference 做出推斷

It turns out that our analysis is particularly well-suited to help us <u>draw an inference</u> about this situation.
事實證明，我們的分析特別適合幫助我們對這種情況做出推斷。

draw + comparison 做比較

I am not sure if one can <u>draw a comparison between</u> the economic impact of COVID-19 and that of the Great Depression.
我不確定是否可以拿 COVID-19 和經濟大蕭條造成的經濟影響做比較。

draw + distinction 區別、區分

The Trump administration attempted to <u>draw a distinction between</u> the Chinese Communist Party and the Chinese people, and made clear that the United States is confronting the former.

川普政府試圖區分中國共產黨和中國人民，並明確表示美國所對峙的為前者。

draw + parallel 做對照、比較

The author of the book <u>draws a parallel</u> between the fall of the Berlin Wall in 1989 and the Arab spring of 2011.

這本書的作者將 1989 年的柏林圍牆倒塌與 2011 年的阿拉伯之春做了比較。

draw + criticism 受到批評

The latest movie <u>drew heavy criticism</u>, both from the general public and from film critics.

這部最新的電影受到大眾和影評人的嚴厲批評。

draw + praise 受到稱讚

The operation of the Taoyuan Metro Line has <u>drawn praise from</u> business leaders and local officials.

桃園機場捷運的營運受到商界領袖和當地官員的稱讚。

實用短語 / 用法 / 句型

1. draw a blank 未能回答、毫無回應

When asked about the news, the city mayor <u>drew a blank</u>.

被問到這個新聞時，市長並未做出回應。

2. draw a line 區隔、劃清界線

Adolescents often use drugs simply to try to <u>draw a line between</u> their own and their parents' way of life.

青少年吸毒經常只是為了試圖在自己和父母的生活方式之間做出區隔。

3. draw the line 拒絕接受、反對～

I don't mind paying employees a high salary, but I <u>draw the line at</u> the notion of being paid for unused sick days. You shouldn't expect to be paid for not getting ill.

我不介意給員工高薪，但對於把沒用完的病假換成薪水，我是堅決反對的。你不應該期望沒生病還能拿錢。

4. draw the eye 吸睛、使人注意到～

With ideas in the banner, the designer used strong contrasts to <u>draw the eye to</u> specific places rather than the whole image.

設計師將想法呈現在橫幅中，並運用強烈的對比將注意力吸引到特定位置，而不是放在整個圖像上。

5. draw to a(n) close / end 接近尾聲、快要結束

As the first half <u>drew to a close</u>, the Warriors quickly extended their lead to 56-43.

上半場接近尾聲時，勇士隊迅速將領先優勢擴大到 56-43。

Drop

▶ MP3-024

(drop — dropped — dropped)

drop + note 留個紙條、留言

I just wanted to <u>drop a note</u> to thank you for making this data available to us.
我想留個紙條感謝你把這些資料提供給我們。

drop + line 留個訊息、留言

If any point interests you in particular, <u>drop me a line</u> below. I'll try to explain.
如果你對某個觀點特別有興趣的話，在底下留言給我，我會試著解釋看看。

drop + hint 給提示、透露線索

I can't wait to see your movie. Do you mind sharing just a little bit and <u>drop us a hint</u>? So we can get excited for that, too.
我等不及想看你的電影了。你介意跟我們分享一下、透露一點消息嗎？我們也可以為此感到興奮。

drop + class / course 退課、退選課程

If I were you, I would <u>drop the course</u> and find an online course somewhere else.
如果我是你，我會退掉這門課，去別的地方找一個線上課程。

drop + price 降價

Apple <u>dropped the price of</u> the iPhone 11 from $699 down to $599 after the company announced the new iPhone 12 series.

在宣布推出新的 iPhone 12 系列之後，蘋果將 iPhone 11 的價格從 699 美元降到 599 美元。

drop + idea 放棄想法、打消念頭

After glimpsing a few price tags, I <u>dropped the idea of</u> shopping.

看了幾個標價後，我打消了購物的念頭。

實用短語 / 用法 / 句型

1. drop the ball 失誤、犯錯、把事情搞砸

In today's world, the US and China will also be impacted if European leaders <u>drop the ball</u>.

在當今的世界，如果歐洲領導人出了錯，美國和中國也會受到影響。

2. drop a bombshell 拋下震撼彈（震驚的消息）

Earlier this month, Microsoft <u>dropped a bombshell</u> in the gaming industry.

這個月初，微軟對遊戲產業拋下一顆震撼彈。

3. drop the subject 停止話題、不說了

As she came back, we <u>dropped the subject</u> and acted like nothing happened.

當她回來時，我們就停止了這個話題，裝作什麼都沒發生。

4. one's jaw dropped 嚇到下巴都快掉下來

<u>My jaw dropped</u> when seeing that my parents come up on the screen.

當我看到父母出現在螢幕上，我嚇到下巴都快掉下來了。

Others

dampen + enthusiasm 澆熄熱情

If the interest rates rise too high, it will <u>dampen</u> investors' <u>enthusiasm</u> and slow the recovery.
如果利率升太高，將澆熄投資人的熱情並減緩復甦。

dampen + spirits 打擊心情

Psychologists say that exposure to bad news can <u>dampen our spirits</u> and sense of hope.
心理學家說，聽到壞消息會打擊我們的心情和希望。

dash + hopes 打破希望、讓希望破滅

The rising number of COVID-19 cases is set to <u>dash hopes of</u> locked-down areas being given more freedom.
COVID-19 病例不斷增加，這將使封城地區獲得更多自由的希望破滅。

disclose + information 透露資訊

She never <u>disclosed information about</u> her patients or gave specifics about her day at work.
她從不透露病人的資訊，也不透露自己工作的具體狀況。

disclose + identity 揭露身分

No other personal information is collected. This allows you to use our website without having to <u>disclose your identity</u>, unless you decide to do so.
其他個人資訊不會被收集。除非您決定要這樣做，否則您可以在不揭露身分的情況下使用我們的網站。

divert + attention 轉移注意力

Through advertising and promotional campaigns, the tobacco industry continues to <u>divert attention from</u> the deadly effects of its products.
透過廣告和促銷活動，菸草業繼續轉移大眾對其產品致命影響的注意。

實用短語 / 用法 / 句型

1. drive a hard bargain 討價還價

Consumers may be inclined to embrace the latest technology, but they're likely to <u>drive a hard bargain on</u> the price.
消費者可能傾向於採用最新技術，但是他們可能會在費用上討價還價。

Eliminate

(eliminate — eliminated — eliminated)

eliminate + discrimination 消除歧視

The advocacy organization has been trying to <u>eliminate sexual orientation discrimination</u> in the workplace.
這個倡議團體一直在努力消除職場的性向歧視。

eliminate + poverty 消除貧困

Participants in this project will examine the causes of poverty, define community resources and explore ways to <u>eliminate poverty</u>.
這個計畫的參與者將研究造成貧困的原因、界定社區資源，並探討消除貧困的方法。

eliminate + barrier 排除阻礙、消除壁壘

The scheme aims to reduce delivery time and cost, <u>eliminate trade barriers</u>, and integrate small markets.
這個計畫的目標是減少運送時間和成本、消除貿易壁壘，並整合小市場。

eliminate + need 消除需求、不再需要

Advances in medical science have <u>eliminated the need for</u> many patients to spend long periods of time in hospital.
醫學的進步使許多病人不再需要長時間待在醫院。

eliminate + necessity 消除必要性

Mobile check-in will <u>eliminate the necessity of</u> human interaction at the times of pandemic.
疫情爆發期間，行動簽到裝置將減少人與人互動的必要性。

eliminate + problem 解決問題、問題不再存在

He supposes that advances in educational technology will <u>eliminate the problem of</u> scarcity of teachers in rural areas.
他認為教育科技的進步，將解決偏鄉地區教師資源短缺的問題。

eliminate + risk 消除風險

The pharmaceutical industry may need FDA regulation in order to <u>eliminate the risk to</u> consumer safety.
醫藥產業可能需要受食藥署的監管，以消除對消費者安全造成的風險。

eliminate + possibility 消除可能性

He needs chemotherapy to <u>eliminate the possibility</u> that the cancer will recur and spread in the future.
他需要進行化療，以消除將來癌症復發和擴散的可能性。

eliminate + use 不再使用

We will have to <u>eliminate the use of</u> fossil fuels and adopt more environmentally sustainable methods.
我們需要杜絕使用化石燃料，並採用更永續環保的方法。

eliminate + requirement 排除要求

The pre-boarding testing will not <u>eliminate the requirement</u> that people arriving in the country quarantine for 14 days.
登機前的檢測，並不會免除入境人員須隔離 14 天的要求。

eliminate + threat 消除威脅

Vaccination of children will reduce but not <u>eliminate the threat of</u> disease transmission.
兒童接種疫苗將會減少，但不會完全消除掉疾病傳播的威脅。

Embrace

▶ MP3-027

(embrace — embraced — embraced)

embrace + diversity 擁抱多樣性、差異

We recruit from all backgrounds and actively <u>embrace cultural diversity</u>.
我們招募各種背景的人才，並積極擁抱文化多樣性。

embrace + technology 擁抱科技

To appeal to potential young talent, traditional industries must market themselves more creatively and <u>embrace technology</u>.
為了吸引有潛力的年輕人才，傳統產業必須更有創意地行銷自己並擁抱科技。

embrace + change 擁抱、接受改變

The more you <u>embrace change</u>, the more comfortable you become with uncertainty and risk.
你越是接受變化，你就越能坦然面對不確定性和風險。

embrace + idea 接受想法、觀念

Can patients <u>embrace the idea</u> that the most expensive care is not always the best care?
病人能否接受，最貴的治療不一定是最好的治療這種想法？

embrace + notion 接受想法、觀念

I think we always have to <u>embrace the notion</u> that great isn't good enough.
我認為我們應該時時抱著「沒有最好，只有更好」的想法。

embrace + challenge 擁抱、接受挑戰

For me, climbing the mountain is not to plant the flag, but to <u>embrace the challenge</u>, enjoy the air, and behold the view.
對我來說，登山不是為了插旗，而是要擁抱挑戰、享受空氣和欣賞美景。

embrace + concept 接受概念

While most restaurant owners and residents I spoke to had heard of World Vegetarian Day, few <u>embraced the concept</u>.
雖然我採訪過的大多數餐廳老闆和居民都聽說過世界素食日，但很少人接受這個概念。

embrace + future 擁抱未來

When you choose to <u>embrace the future</u>, you will view everything you encounter as an opportunity for growth.
當你選擇擁抱未來時，你會把遇到的每件事都看成是成長的機會。

Exercise

(exercise — exercised — exercised)

exercise + caution 小心謹慎

Traffic in Taiwan moves along the right side of the road.
Visitors from Singapore and Hong Kong should be aware
that traffic is on the opposite side of the road and should
<u>exercise caution</u>.
在臺灣，車輛靠右行駛。新加坡和香港的旅客應注意車流是不同方
向、小心行走。

exercise + discretion 行使決定權、裁量權

The police <u>exercise discretion</u> in the area of minor traffic
offenses.
警察在輕微違規事件上有自由裁量權。

exercise + right 行使權利

Young voters have launched crowdfunding campaigns
to rent buses in order to take college students home to
<u>exercise their civil rights</u> and vote for presidential elections.
年輕選民發起群眾募資活動，租遊覽車送大學生回家行使公民權，
為總統選舉投票。

A
B
C
D
E
F
G
H
I
J
K
L
M
N
O
P
Q
R
S
T
U
V
W

exercise + power 行使權力

Brand is extremely important in maintaining and growing market share in a world where consumers can <u>exercise the power of</u> choice with a simple click of the mouse.
在一個消費者只需簡單點擊滑鼠就能行使選擇權的世界裡，品牌對於維持和增加市場佔有率極度重要。

exercise + control 控制

The Chinese Communist Party <u>exercises control over</u> many multinational companies in China.
中國共產黨控制著許多在中國的跨國公司。

exercise + influence 施加影響

He is not on the board of directors, and he doesn't <u>exercise influence over</u> the investment decisions.
他不是董事會成員，不會影響公司的投資決策。

exercise + authority 行使職權、權力

For fear of losing their supporters, many politicians are afraid to <u>exercise their authority</u>.
由於害怕失去支持者，許多政客不敢行使自己的職權。

exercise + discipline 遵守紀律

Used wisely, credit cards can be convenient, particularly for people who <u>exercise discipline</u> and pay their balances in full each month.

好好使用的話，信用卡是很方便的，尤其是對於那些遵守紀律、每月全額繳清的人來說。

Exert

(exert — exerted — exerted)

exert + influence 發揮、施加影響

There's no doubt that our peers <u>exert enormous influence on</u> our behavior.
毫無疑問地，同儕對我們的行為有很大的影響。

exert + pressure 施加壓力

Environmental groups are <u>exerting pressure on</u> the government to tighten pollution laws.
環保團體正在向政府施壓，要求政府嚴格加強污染法規。

exert + control 控制

In democracies, the government will not interfere or <u>exert control over</u> day-to-day company operations.
在民主國家，政府不會干預或控制公司的日常營運。

exert + effort 付出努力、盡力

The prime minister promised that she will <u>exert every effort to</u> outline the benefits of a future trade deal that will be in the national interest and protect jobs and the economy.
總理承諾，她將盡一切努力列出未來貿易協定的好處，它會符合國家利益，並保障就業和經濟。

exert + power 施加影響

China continues to invest abroad in its drive to secure access to natural resources in places like Afghanistan and Australia and to <u>exert power</u> in these places.
中國繼續在海外投資，以確保能獲得阿富汗和澳洲等地的自然資源，並對這些國家施加影響。

exert + force 施力

It's not possible for objects to <u>exert a force on</u> each other while remaining stationary.
物體不可能在保持靜止的情況下對彼此施力。

exert + authority 行使職權、權力

The report shows that the administration refused to <u>exert its authority on</u> the rioters that broke into the Congress building.
報告顯示，政府拒絕對闖入國會大廈的暴徒行使公權力。

Expand

▶ MP3-030

(expand — expanded — expanded)

expand + horizons　拓展視野

If you have been looking for something different to learn to expand your horizons, this working holiday program may suit you.

如果你一直在尋找一些不同的東西來學習，以拓展你的視野，那麼這個打工度假計畫可能適合你。

expand + knowledge　拓展知識

Why not set some goals about future travel plans or ways to expand your knowledge?

為什麼不設定一些關於未來旅行計畫的目標或拓展知識的方法呢？

expand + opportunity　擴大、增加機會

These techniques are also taught to students to practice at home to expand opportunities for learning.

這些技術也會教給學生，讓他們在家裡練習，以增加學習的機會。

expand + vocabulary　增加字彙量

There are many ways to expand your vocabulary, but the quickest and most effective way to develop an improved vocabulary is to start with the words you currently use.

有很多方法可以增加你的字彙量，但是最快、最有效提升字彙量的方法是從你現在使用的單字著手。

expand + capacity 擴大產能

In practice, we want to <u>expand capacity</u> when demand grows sufficiently. Thus, the point is to determine when the growth meets the criterion to justify extra capacity.

實際上，我們希望在需求增加夠多時擴大產能。因此，重點在於決定成長的幅度何時達到擴大產能的標準。

expand + operations 擴大營運、規模

In these trying times, businesses would have less money to <u>expand operations</u>, add new jobs and raise wages.

在這艱困的時期，企業用於擴大業務、增加新職缺和調薪的資金將減少。

expand + number 擴大、增加數量

The university is planning to <u>expand the number of</u> students to over 20,000.

該大學正計劃將學生人數增加到 2 萬人以上。

expand + coverage 擴大涵蓋範圍

The government is dedicated to <u>expanding coverage</u> and improving the quality of healthcare services.

政府致力於擴大健康照護服務涵蓋的範圍和提升健康照護的品質。

實用短語 / 用法 / 句型

1. expand the scope of 擴大範圍

A primary goal of the project is to <u>expand the scope of</u> discussion on applications of artificial intelligence in elderly care robots.

這個專案的主要目標為擴大討論人工智慧在老人照護機器人上的應用。

Evade

▶ MP3-031

(evade — evaded — evaded)

evade + tax 逃稅

The day before, he and a bunch of senior colleagues were arrested for helping big companies <u>evade tax</u>.
就在前一天，他和一群資深同事因協助大公司逃稅而被捕。

evade + law 逃避法律

Registering the company abroad is the reason they have been able to <u>evade the law</u> for this long.
註冊境外公司是他們長期以來能夠逃避法律制裁的原因。

evade + responsibilities 逃避責任

It is natural for many persons to seek to <u>evade their responsibilities</u> and avoid their duties.
對許多人來說，想逃避責任和義務是很自然的。

evade + question 迴避問題

The best interviewers and podcasters make it difficult for politicians to <u>evade questions</u>.
厲害的採訪者和 podcast 主持人讓政客們很難迴避問題。

evade + issue 逃避問題、議題

This was felt by many residents as a deliberate attempt to <u>evade the important issue of</u> protecting the field for future generations to enjoy.

許多居民認為，這是在故意逃避保護這片土地供後代使用的重要議題。

evade + capture 躲避追捕

By the time of his capture, the criminal had managed to <u>evade capture</u> for more than four days.

犯人被逮時，他已經躲了超過 4 天的追捕。

Others

▶ MP3-032

enlist + help 尋求協助、幫忙

Golfers nowadays often <u>enlist the help of</u> computers in an effort to improve their game.
現在的高爾夫球選手經常借助電腦來提升球技。

enlist + support 尋求協助、支持

I hope you can <u>enlist the support</u> and practical help of your parents and some of your teachers. No one should worry about regularly being made fun of.
我希望你能向父母和一些老師尋求支持和實際協助，沒有人應該擔心經常被人取笑。

enlist + aid 尋求協助、幫忙

For adults, we might suggest that you <u>enlist the aid of</u> a career counselor to help you find an ideal job.
對於成年人，我們會建議你尋求職涯顧問的幫忙，協助你找到一份理想的工作。

enlist + services 尋求服務、協助

Some businesses <u>enlist the services of</u> psychologists in order to retain employees and maintain their good work ethic.
一些企業為了留住員工以及保持他們良好的職業道德，而尋求心理學家的協助。

exfoliate + skin 去除角質

This product is an excellent way to help you <u>exfoliate the skin</u> once a week before bed.
這個產品是幫助你每週一次在睡前去角質的好方法。

expose + truth 揭露真相

The new book <u>exposes the truth about</u> the financial institution bailouts during the 2008 financial crisis.
這本新書揭露了有關 2008 年金融危機期間金融機構紓困的真相。

expose + corruption 揭發弊端、腐敗

In the mass market, tabloids play a vital role in British life. They <u>expose corruption</u> and hold politicians' feet to the fire.
在大眾市場中，小報在英國人的生活扮演重要角色。它們揭露弊端、對政客施壓。

Facilitate

▶ MP3-033

(facilitate — facilitated — facilitated)

facilitate + communication 促進溝通

We are supposed to <u>facilitate communication</u> and get everybody to speak up.
我們應該促進溝通、讓每個人暢所欲言。

facilitate + discussion 促進討論

If you're leading a presentation, part of your job is to <u>facilitate discussion</u> and make it easier for people to participate.
如果你要主持一場簡報，你的工作之一就是促進討論、並使大家更容易參與。

facilitate + exchange 促進交換、交流

Although the Internet can <u>facilitate the exchange of</u> information, much of the information displayed to users is unfiltered and even biased.
雖然網路可以促進資訊交流，但呈現給使用者的許多資訊是未經過濾，甚至帶有偏見的。

A
B
C
D
E
F
G
H
I
J
K
L
M
N
O
P
Q
R
S
T
U
V
W

facilitate + development 促進發展

In the future, the new analytical methods will <u>facilitate the development of</u> biomedical engineering.
在未來，新的分析方法將促進生物醫學工程的發展。

facilitate + use 促進使用、應用

The master's program will offer you more opportunities for personal growth and also <u>facilitate the use of</u> psychological principles for effective leadership.
碩士課程將提供你更多個人成長的機會，並促進心理學原理的應用，達到有效的領導。

facilitate + collaboration 促進合作

Our goal is to <u>facilitate collaboration</u> across multiple functions, departments and levels.
我們的目標是促進跨職責、跨部門和跨層級的合作。

facilitate + transition 促進移交、交接

I would be glad to extend my assistance to <u>facilitate the transition of</u> the work to the next consultant if needed.
如果有需要，我很樂意提供協助，以利將工作交接給下一位顧問。

facilitate + transfer 促進轉換

The role of a teacher is to provide instructions that will not only facilitate learning but also <u>facilitate the transfer of</u> acquired knowledge and skills beyond the initial learning context.

老師的角色不只是提供指導來促進學習，更是促進知識及技能在原先學習環境外的轉換。

facilitate + process 促使過程發生、順利進行

If we can <u>facilitate the process</u>, we can dramatically increase productivity and efficiency, and reduce our marginal cost.

如果我們可以使這個過程順利進行，我們就能大大提高生產力和效率，並降低邊際成本。

facilitate + learning 促進學習

The role of a teacher is to <u>facilitate learning</u>. However, part of the problem is that the dominant culture of education has come to focus not on teaching and learning, but on testing.

老師的作用是促進學習。但是部分問題在於，教育的主流文化已經不再注重教學與學習，而是注重考試。

facilitate + access 促使～更容易取得

Online learning platforms, such as Coursera and Udemy, <u>facilitate access to</u> knowledge and learning resources, particularly for students in rural areas.

Coursera 和 Udemy 這類的線上學習平台，讓知識和學習資源更容易取得，特別是對偏鄉地區的學生而言。

Field

▶ MP3-034

(field — fielded — fielded)

field + question 回答提問（特別指有很多或是不好回答的問題）

The head coach and key players will <u>field questions from</u> the press in this room after the game.
比賽結束後，總教練和主力球員將在這個房間回答媒體的提問。

field + inquiry 回答詢問（特別指有很多或是不好回答的問題）

Putting poorly trained employees on a telephone and expecting them to <u>field customer inquiries</u> is risky. In fact, that may only make matters worse.
讓沒有受過良好訓練的員工接電話、回答顧客的問題是有風險的。事實上，那可能只會讓事情變得更糟。

field + call 接聽電話（特別指有很多或是不好回答的問題）

The overall goal of this department is to <u>field phone calls</u>, put together information and then to refer business to the appropriate experts.
這個部門的整體目標是接聽電話、彙整資訊，然後將業務轉介給合適的專家。

field + team 成立、組織團隊

The school didn't <u>field a basketball team</u> last year because of a lack of funds.
由於缺乏資金，學校去年沒有成立籃球隊。

field + lineup 組織陣容

Despite Stephen Curry's injury crisis, the Warriors <u>fielded a</u> balanced <u>lineup</u> with multiple scoring threats.

儘管 Stephen Curry 出現傷病危機，但勇士隊組織了一個戰力平均、有多個得分點的陣容。

field + candidate 推派候選人

The big question is whether the new party can reach a consensus in time to <u>field candidates</u> in this election.

最大的問題是，這個新政黨能否及時達成共識，以便在這次選舉中推派出候選人。

File

(file — filed — filed)

file + complaint 投訴、申訴

If negligence causes death, it is likely that your first instinct is to <u>file a complaint against</u> the doctor.
如果因過失導致死亡，你的第一反應可能是投訴醫生。

file + claim 索取賠償

They say they have <u>filed a claim with</u> the company for damage to their basement caused by sewage water.
他們說已經就污水對地下室造成的毀損向該公司索取賠償。

file + lawsuit 提起訴訟、提告

If no action is taken in the next 60 days, the shop owner said he would <u>file a lawsuit</u>.
如果在接下來的 60 天內沒有採取任何行動，老闆表示將提起訴訟。

file + petition 遞交訴狀、提出請願

Opponents have <u>filed a petition</u>, seeking a referendum to overturn the change in law.
反對者已經提交了一份請願書，希望透過公投來推翻法律的修改。

file + report 提交報告

A penalty is imposed for failure to <u>file a report</u> or provide the Financial Supervisory Commission with required information in the report.
如果未提交報告或未在報告中向金管會提供必要的資訊，將被處以罰鍰。

file + return 提交稅表、報稅

Though most people <u>file returns</u> electronically, we still received nearly six million paper returns last year.
雖然大多數的人都是電子報稅，但去年我們還是收了近 600 萬份的紙本稅表。

Fill

(fill — filled — filled)

---

fill + gap 彌補落差、不足

The scheme is aimed at <u>filling the gap in</u> people's real-life driving skills before they actually take to the road.
本計畫目標在補足民眾真正開車上路前，對於現實生活中駕駛能力的不足。

---

fill + need 滿足需求

The grant program was created to <u>fill the need for</u> qualified teachers in remote areas.
為滿足偏鄉地區對於合格教師的需求，設立了這個補助計畫。

---

fill + demand 滿足需求

In order to <u>fill the demand for</u> labor, many large technology companies are seeking workers from other countries.
為了滿足人力需求，許多大型科技公司開始招聘外國員工。

---

fill + niche 滿足利基、潛在需求

A frequent complaint among independent travelers is tour packages are sometimes too touristy. To resolve this issue, some travel startups have built platforms to <u>fill the niche</u> in the market.
自助旅行者常有的抱怨是套裝行程有時太過觀光化。為了解決這個問題，一些旅遊新創公司建立了平台來滿足這個市場的潛在需求。

fill + order　供應訂貨

As long as we give the factories a heads up a couple days in advance, they can usually <u>fill the order</u>.
只要我們提前幾天通知工廠，他們通常可以供貨。

fill + void　彌補不足；填補失落感

The amusement park will <u>fill a void</u> in this town, which has little entertainment for children.
這個遊樂園將彌補鎮上兒童娛樂活動的不足。

fill + vacancy　填補空缺

Nowadays skilled workers are few in Taiwan, and employers are having trouble <u>filling vacancies</u>.
現今臺灣的技術工人很少，雇主很難填補空缺。

fill + position　填補空缺、職位

We are currently seeking qualified candidates to <u>fill the position of</u> Project Manager.
我們目前正在尋找符合資格的人選來填補專案經理的職缺。

fill + role　擔負、擔任角色

I think ebooks will be popular because there is a certain need for them, but they will never <u>fill the role of</u> paper books, especially for the feel of a book.
我認為電子書會很流行，因為人們對它有一定的需求，但它們永遠無法取代紙本書，尤其是在書的觸感上。

fill + time / days 找事情打發時間、在空檔安排事情做

Travelers to Tainan are mostly there for street food, so they don't need a package tour in the way of helping them <u>fill their days</u>.

去臺南玩的遊客大多是衝著小吃去的,所以他們應該不需要跟團來安排行程。

實用短語 / 用法 / 句型

1. fill the bill 符合要求

Thinking over a selection of cars, I concluded that this one <u>fills the bill</u> perfectly. It's cheap and gets good mileage.

在挑了幾款車後,我的結論是這款車完全符合需求,它既便宜又省油。

2. fill one's shoes 接替、取代某人的位置

No one can <u>fill Steve Jobs' shoes</u>, but many young entrepreneurs work to follow in his footsteps.

沒有人可以取代 Steve Jobs 的位置,但許多年輕企業家都在努力追隨他的腳步。

Fix

▶ MP3-037

(fix — fixed — fixed)

fix + bug 修復系統漏洞

After learning of the attack, Microsoft released a software patch to <u>fix the bug</u> on the same day.
得知這次的攻擊後，微軟在同一天釋出了一個軟體修補程式來修復該漏洞。

fix + error 修復錯誤

If you try to download an app from the App Store and it doesn't work, <u>fix the error</u> with the following troubleshooting steps.
如果你嘗試從 App Store 下載應用程式，但無法正常運作，請按照以下的故障排除步驟來修復錯誤。

fix + problem 解決問題

The purpose of today's meeting is to discuss how to <u>fix the problem</u> without causing a panic among investors.
今天會議的目的是討論如何解決問題，而不會引起投資人的恐慌。

A
B
C
D
E
F
G
H
I
J
K
L
M
N
O
P
Q
R
S
T
U
V
W

fix + issue 解決問題

After two hours of heated discussion, the decision was made not to <u>fix the issue</u> directly but to provide a workaround.
經過兩個小時的熱烈討論後，決定不直接解決此問題，而是提供一個替代方案。

fix + date 訂下日期

Due to the COVID-19 pandemic, we haven't <u>fixed a firm date for</u> our wedding in Taiwan.
由於 COVID-19 疫情的關係，我們還沒確定在臺灣舉辦婚禮的日期。

fix + time 訂下時間

Shall we <u>fix a time for</u> our next meeting? We'll come to a final conclusion then.
我們訂個下次開會的時間好嗎？我們到時會做出最後結論。

fix + price 訂定統一的價格（通常是為了達到價格上的壟斷，來提高賣方的利潤）

The two big companies are accused of <u>fixing the price of</u> milk, trying to eliminate competition in the dairy market.
這兩家大公司被指控控制牛奶價格，試圖消除乳品市場的競爭。

實用短語 / 用法 / 句型

1. fix one's attention / eyes on sth 把注意力、目光集中在～上

I tried to ignore the constant dings from my phone and <u>fix all my attention on</u> the work at hand.

我試圖忽略手機不斷傳來的通知聲，把所有注意力集中在手邊的工作上。

Follow

▶ MP3-038

(follow — followed — followed)

follow + instructions 遵從指示

If you're not feeling well or showing symptoms that might be associated with COVID-19, you should seek medical attention and <u>follow the instructions of</u> your healthcare provider.

如果你感覺不舒服或出現疑似 COVID-19 的症狀，你應該就醫，並遵從醫護人員的指示。

follow + steps 按照步驟

If you want a chance to get a free movie ticket, all you have to do is <u>follow the steps</u> below.

如果想要有機會獲得一張免費的電影票，你只需要按照下面的步驟做。

follow + procedure 遵照程序

All you had to do was <u>follow the correct procedure</u>, and none of this damage would have occurred.

你要做的就是遵照正確程序，這樣就不會造成這種傷害了。

follow + guidelines 遵守準則

All foreign nationals will be expected to <u>follow the guidelines</u> issued by the Central Epidemic Command Center.

所有外籍人士都要遵守中央流行疫情指揮中心發布的指導準則。

follow + directions 按照說明、指示

People who take frozen meals to work should <u>follow the directions</u> closely <u>for</u> heating.
帶冷凍食品來公司的人應嚴格遵守加熱指示。

follow + rule 遵守規定

Any foreign company that would like to do business and stay in China should <u>follow the rule of</u> the Communist Party of China.
任何想在中國做生意、並留下來的外國公司，都應該遵守中國共產黨的規定。

follow + advice 聽從建議

It requires all of us—the entire country—to <u>follow the advice of</u> experts and practice social distancing to keep the epidemic under control.
這需要我們所有人，也就是整個國家，都聽從專家的建議，保持社交距離，以控制疫情。

follow + lead 仿效

Environmentalists are urging the government to <u>follow the lead of</u> European countries in using more renewable energy.
環保人士呼籲政府仿效歐洲國家使用更多的再生能源。

follow + example 仿效做法

Some public schools <u>follow the example of</u> private schools in asking parents to donate money.
一些公立學校仿效私立學校的做法，要求家長捐款。

follow + pattern 遵循模式

Most Taiwanese people prefer California to New York, for the weather on the West Coast <u>follows a</u> fairly predictable <u>pattern</u>.
比起紐約，大多數臺灣人更喜歡加州，因為西岸的天氣很規律且好預測。

實用短語 / 用法 / 句型

1. follow suit 仿效

The budget airline has been so successful that other traditional airlines have to <u>follow suit</u> and lower their fares.
廉價航空公司如此成功，以至於其他傳統航空公司不得不跟進並降低票價。

2. follow in one's footsteps 追隨某人的腳步

He plans to <u>follow in the footsteps of</u> his father, who has devoted his 30-year career to improving the quality of healthcare in resource-poor settings.
他計劃追隨父親的腳步，他父親 30 年的職業生涯都致力於改善資源匱乏地區的醫療品質。

Formulate

(formulate — formulated — formulated)

formulate + plan 制定計畫

With these considerations in mind, you can work with your doctor to <u>formulate a plan</u> to treat your migraine headaches.
考量到這些因素，你可以和你的醫生一起制定一個治療偏頭痛的計畫。

formulate + theory 提出理論

Ever since Einstein <u>formulated the</u> general <u>theory of</u> relativity, which links gravity, space and time, physicists have been trying to test its predictions.
自從愛因斯坦提出將重力、空間和時間連結起來的廣義相對論以後，物理學家們一直在嘗試驗證他的預測。

formulate + policy 制定政策

It always takes time for a president to put his team in place, <u>formulate policies</u>, steer legislation through Congress and conduct foreign negotiations.
總統總是需要時間來安排自己的團隊、制定政策、引導國會通過立法、以及進行外交談判。

formulate + strategy 制定策略

The company has hired a financial adviser to assist in
<u>formulating a</u> growth <u>strategy</u>.
該公司已聘請一位財務顧問來協助制定成長策略。

formulate + rules 制定規則

Negotiators from 50 countries are meeting to <u>formulate
rules for</u> governing cross-border lawsuits.
來自 50 個國家的談判代表，正在開會制定管理跨境訴訟的規則。

formulate + proposal 制定方案、計畫

The government has set up a working group to <u>formulate
proposals for</u> reducing environmental pollution.
政府已經成立了一個工作小組，以制定減少環境污染的計畫。

formulate + question 組織、提出問題

My advisor coached me into a better job by helping me
<u>formulate</u> appropriate <u>questions for</u> my potential boss.
我的顧問教我對未來的老闆提出好的問題，來幫助我找到一份更好
的工作。

formulate + response 組織、提出回答

In addition to buying time to <u>formulate the</u> best <u>response</u>, the witness' delay in responses also gave the judge the impression that he was thoughtful in his answers.
除了爭取時間組織最好的回答外，證人的延遲答覆也讓法官留下印象，認為他的回答是經過深思熟慮的。

formulate + recommendation 提出建議

We split into groups to try to <u>formulate recommendations on</u> such issues as nutrition, education and transportation.
我們分成幾個小組，試著就營養、教育和交通等議題提出建議。

formulate + idea 組織、提出想法

In practice, every opportunity should be taken to encourage students to <u>formulate ideas</u> for themselves.
實際上，應該利用每一個機會來鼓勵學生提出自己的想法。

formulate + hypothesis 提出假設

In the activity, students can learn to <u>formulate a hypothesis</u> and test it.
在這個活動中，學生們可以學習提出假設並驗證。

Foster

(foster — fostered — fostered)

foster + development 促進發展

The Bill and Melinda Gates Foundation pledged $55 million over six years to <u>foster the development of</u> a vaccine for dengue fever and stop its global spread.
蓋茲基金會承諾在 6 年內投入 5500 萬美元，促進登革熱疫苗的開發並阻止其在全球的傳播。

foster + growth 促進成長

Apple believes that keeping the price of new songs low will <u>foster the growth of</u> the online music market.
蘋果認為，維持較低的新歌價格，可以促進線上音樂市場的成長。

foster + use 促進使用

One of the aims of the project is to <u>foster the use of</u> educational technology in public schools.
該計畫的目的之一，是促進教育科技在公立學校中的應用。

foster + idea 養成觀念、想法

Not all problems children have can be attributed to their parents, though regrettably the general public have <u>fostered this idea</u> that parents are largely to blame.
並非兒童所有的問題都可以歸咎於他們的父母，但遺憾的是大眾已經養成了這個觀念，認為父母要負起很大的責任。

foster + innovation 促進創新

Social media platforms have huge potential to <u>foster innovation</u> in businesses of any size.
社群平台擁有巨大的潛力，可以促進大大小小企業的創新。

foster + creativity 培養創造力

We appreciate a leader who can <u>foster creativity</u> and get the employees to talk to each other.
我們欣賞能培養創造力並促進員工互相交流的領導者。

foster + communication 促進溝通

The upper management intends to host forums with all staff to <u>foster better communication</u> in the organization.
高階管理人員打算與所有員工一起舉辦論壇，以促進組織內部更好的溝通。

foster + exchange 促進交流

These collaboration agreements will improve the effectiveness of cooperation in the field of renewable energy and <u>foster the exchange of</u> scientific information.
這些合作協議將提高再生能源領域合作的效果，並促進科學資訊的交流。

A
B
C
D
E
F
G
H
I
J
K
L
M
N
O
P
Q
R
S
T
U
V
W

foster + relationships 促進關係

The system attempts to <u>foster relationships between</u> hospitals and clinical research teams to find the best ways to care for patients.
這個系統試圖促進醫院和臨床研究團隊的關係，以找到照顧病人的最佳方法。

foster + integration 促進融合、整合

Some politicians and commentators say a stronger sense of shared American values is needed to <u>foster integration of</u> immigrants into US society.
一些政治人物和評論家表示，要促進移民融入美國社會，就需要有更強烈的共同美國價值。

foster + collaboration 促進合作

To <u>foster collaboration</u>, our work space is open, with no partitions, doors, or closed-off glass offices.
為了促進合作，我們的工作空間是開放式的，沒有隔板、沒有門、也沒有封閉式的玻璃辦公室。

foster + competition 促進競爭、提高競爭力

The telecom company wants to <u>foster competition in</u> the Internet services market and keep prices low for consumers.
這家電信公司希望提升網路服務市場的競爭力，並為消費者維持低價。

Others

▶ MP3-041

---

flip + coin 丟硬幣（通常是在兩個選項之間猶豫不決時所做）

The kid must <u>flip a coin</u> to decide between the Batman and the Superman outfit for tonight's Halloween party.
孩子必須擲硬幣來決定，今晚萬聖節派對是要穿蝙蝠俠裝還是超人裝。

---

forge + consensus 達成共識

The governments and environmentalists took the lead several years ago in trying to <u>forge a consensus on</u> climate change.
幾年前，各國政府和環保人士率先試圖在氣候變遷議題上達成共識。

---

forge + relationship 建立關係

One of the powerful things about technology and the Internet right now is you can <u>forge relationships with</u> people around the globe.
現在科技和網路強大的功能之一是，你可以與世界各地的人建立關係。

Gain

▶ MP3-042

(gain — gained — gained)

gain + insight 深入了解

We decided to conduct a survey to <u>gain insight into</u> product development, consumer needs, and strategic opportunities.
我們決定進行一項調查，以深入了解產品開發、消費者需求和策略機會。

gain + understanding 了解

At this meeting, parents will have the opportunity to <u>gain a better understanding of</u> the college admissions process.
在這次會議上，家長們將有機會進一步了解大學招生程序。

gain + knowledge 獲得知識

His podcast helps young adults <u>gain knowledge of</u> investment and know what is happening in the market today.
他的 podcast 幫助年輕人獲得投資的知識，並了解現在市場的動向。

gain + access 取得

Some users expressed uncertainty about the new policy, questioning whether Facebook would <u>gain access to</u> private messages or other personal data.

有些用戶對新政策表示不確定，質疑 Facebook 是否會取得私人訊息或其他個人資料。

gain + weight 增重、變胖

We all have our own reasons for working out. It can be to lose weight, to <u>gain weight</u>, to build muscle, to gain self-confidence, or even to relieve stress and anxiety.

我們都有自己健身的理由。它可以是為了減重、增重、增肌、獲得自信、或是減輕壓力和焦慮。

gain + momentum 獲得動力、聲勢

Stand-up comedy began to <u>gain momentum</u> in Taiwan with the opening of some comedy clubs.

隨著一些喜劇俱樂部的成立，單口喜劇在臺灣開始流行起來。

gain + popularity 受歡迎、流行

As ebooks are <u>gaining popularity</u>, they pose a challenge to traditional publishers.

隨著電子書越來越受歡迎，它們對傳統出版商帶來挑戰。

gain + traction （觀念、產品）流行起來、被接受

With growing use among college students, online education is seemingly <u>gaining traction</u> during the COVID-19 pandemic.
隨著越來越多大學生在線上學習，線上教育在 COVID-19 疫情期間似乎流行了起來。

gain + recognition 獲得認可、肯定

Just as in other professions, talented teachers need opportunities to advance their skills and <u>gain recognition</u>.
就像其他行業一樣，有能力的老師需要機會來增進他們的技能並獲得肯定。

gain + reputation 獲得名聲

First released last year, The Queen's Gambit is starting to <u>gain a reputation as</u> a must-see series on Netflix.
去年推出的《后翼棄兵》（The Queen's Gambit）已經成為 Netflix 的必看影集。

gain + exposure 獲得曝光

The podcast industry is growing, and an increasing number of sponsors are happy to pay for the chance to <u>gain exposure for</u> their brands.
podcast 產業正在成長，有越來越多的贊助商願意花錢來換取品牌曝光的機會。

gain + approval 獲得同意、批准

There is nothing new to announce, but we remain positive that the deal will <u>gain approval</u>.

沒有什麼新消息要宣布的,但我們仍保持樂觀,相信這筆交易會獲准。

gain + advantage 獲得優勢

By improving its manufacturing processes and communication with customers, the firm attempts to <u>gain an advantage over</u> its competitors in the industry.

透過改善製作流程以及與顧客的溝通,該公司試圖獲得優勢、超越同業的競爭者。

gain + edge 獲得優勢

By reducing prices, Tesla is looking to <u>gain a competitive edge over</u> its rivals in China.

透過降價的方式,特斯拉希望獲得競爭優勢,超越在中國的競爭對手。

gain + control 控制

The Trump administration have issued a series of policies, trying to <u>gain control of</u> immigration and bring order to the labor market.

川普政府頒布了一系列政策,試圖控制移民、維護勞動力市場的秩序。

gain + support 獲得支持

I believe that your innovative ideas will <u>gain support</u> once they have been further improved upon.
我相信只要你的創新想法能進一步做調整，它們就會受到支持。

實用短語 / 用法 / 句型

1. gain a foothold 取得立足點、站穩腳步

We are reducing trade barriers to help businesses <u>gain a foothold in</u> new markets and providing lower interest rates for small- and medium-sized enterprises.
我們正在降低關稅壁壘，以幫助企業能在新的市場取得立足點，同時也為中小企業提供更低的利率。

Garner

▶ MP3-043

(garner — garnered — garnered)

garner + support 獲得支持

If that documentary was intended to <u>garner support</u> and sympathy <u>for</u> social work, it backfired.
如果這部紀錄片是為了獲得人們對社會工作的支持與同情，那就適得其反了。

garner + attention 獲得關注

Players sometimes <u>garner</u> more <u>attention</u> and praise than they deserve because of the media.
球員們有時會因為媒體而獲得過多的關注和稱讚。

garner + information 獲取資訊

The news media included a questionnaire in their app to <u>garner the information</u> they wanted.
新聞媒體在自己的應用程式中加入了一份問卷，以獲取想要的資訊。

garner + votes 贏得選票

The candidate did not <u>garner</u> enough <u>votes</u> in the primary election to allow his consideration for the office.
候選人在初選階段沒有獲得足夠的票數，因此無法被提名參選。

Gather

▶ MP3-044

(gather — gathered — gathered)

gather + information 收集資料

Sensors are constantly <u>gathering information about</u> performance, vehicle health, and other metrics in today's self-driving cars.

感測器不斷收集關於目前自駕車性能、車輛健康狀況、及其他指標的資料。

gather + data 收集數據

Companies <u>gather data on</u> consumers' buying habits to track product popularity.

公司透過收集消費者購買習慣的數據,來追蹤產品的受歡迎程度。

gather + evidence 蒐集證據

Sometimes lawyers need to <u>gather evidence</u> during the course of a lawsuit because they might not have all of the evidence when starting their particular lawsuit.

有時律師需要在訴訟過程中蒐集證據,因為他們在訴訟開始時可能沒有全部的證據。

Generate

▶ MP3-045

(generate — generated — generated)

generate + electricity 發電

These solar panels <u>generate</u> enough <u>electricity</u> to supply a home with all its energy requirements.
這些太陽能板所產生的電力，足以滿足一個家庭的所有用電需求。

generate + power 發電

There is an urgent need to re-equip the city with new plants to <u>generate power</u> in such adverse weather conditions.
在這種惡劣的天氣條件下，重啟城市新的電廠來發電是當務之急。

generate + revenue 創造收益

The business failed to <u>generate</u> sufficient <u>revenue</u> to cover its operating and capital costs.
該公司未能創造足夠的收入來支付營運和資本成本。

generate + income 創造收入

How the podcaster truly <u>generates income</u> for his business is not through advertising and sponsorship but through his online courses and consulting services.
這位 pocast 主持人為自己的事業創造真正收入的方式，不是透過廣告和贊助，而是透過線上課程和諮詢服務。

generate + sales 帶來銷售量

The new marketing campaign is expected to <u>generate sales</u> during Thanksgiving and Christmas next year.
新的行銷活動預計將在明年感恩節和聖誕節期間帶來銷量。

generate + profits 創造利潤

The moves allowed the hedge fund to avoid losses of \$194 million and <u>generate profits</u> of \$82.8 million.
此舉使這家對沖基金避免了 1.94 億美元的損失，並帶來 8280 萬美元的利潤。

generate + idea 產出點子、想法

Anyone who is interested in applying for this position must be able to organize information, <u>generate original ideas</u>, and solve problems.
對這個職缺有興趣的應徵者，必須具備組織資訊、產出原創性點子和解決問題的能力。

generate + interest 引起興趣

We hope this visual marketing strategy will help us reach more readers and perhaps <u>generate greater interest in</u> the new book.
我們希望這個視覺行銷策略能幫助我們接觸到更多的讀者，或許還能引起讀者對這本新書更大的興趣。

Grab
(grab — grabbed — grabbed)

▶ MP3-046

grab + attention 引起注意

A tweet by Elon Musk, the founder of Tesla, has <u>grabbed the attention of</u> Wall Street traders and investors.
特斯拉創辦人 Elon Musk 的一則推文，引起了華爾街交易員和投資人的注意。

grab + headlines 占據新聞頭條

News about some retirees returning to work with their full salary has <u>grabbed the headlines</u>.
一些退休人員領全薪重返工作崗位的新聞占據了頭版。

grab + opportunity 抓住機會

We've seen again and again that people who put ideas into practice reap rewards. You can't afford to stand still or someone else is going to <u>grab the opportunity</u>.
我們已經一次又一次地看到，把想法付諸實行的人獲得回報。你不能停在原地不動，否則別人就會抓住這個機會往前。

grab + bite 隨便吃點東西（通常是因為時間不多）

We don't have much time to wait, so why not <u>grab a bite</u> from the coffee shop nearby?
我們沒有太多時間可以等待，所以何不去附近的咖啡廳隨便吃點東西？

grab + snack　隨便吃點零食（通常是因為時間不多）

Sorry guys, let me pause the movie and run to the bathroom and <u>grab a snack</u> really quickly.
朋友們，不好意思，讓我先暫停一下電影，快速去個洗手間、隨便找點零食。

grab + lunch　隨便吃個午餐（通常是因為時間不多）

A few others stopped by to join the discussion, and we decided to <u>grab lunch</u> while talking about ideas.
其他幾個人過來加入討論，我們決定隨便吃個午餐邊討論想法。

grab + coffee　買杯咖啡

If you invite him out to <u>grab coffee</u> or a drink, it is going to greatly improve your relationship.
如果你邀他一起出去買杯咖啡或飲料，這將大大改善你們的關係。

grab + drink　喝一杯、喝點東西

When the event came to an end, everyone was looking to <u>grab a drink</u> after the long stressful day.
當活動結束時，每個人都想著在這緊張又漫長的一天後喝一杯。

grab + seat　搶個位子

Could you get there early and <u>grab</u> some <u>good seats</u> for us?
你能早點到幫我們搶個好位子嗎？

實用短語 / 用法 / 句型

1. grab hold of sth 抓住、把握住～

The man <u>grabbed hold of</u> my bag and disappeared quickly into the crowd.

那個人抓了我的袋子，然後很快地消失在人群中。

Grasp

▶ MP3-047

(grasp — grasped — grasped)

grasp + concept 理解概念

Though I have no trouble <u>grasping its concepts</u>, math continues to be difficult for me.
儘管理解數學概念不是問題，但數學對我來說還是很困難。

grasp + idea 理解想法、觀點

Some students find it difficult to <u>grasp the idea</u> that strong economic growth is required to support political clout in international relations.
學生們很難理解在國際關係中，需要強勁的經濟成長來支持政治影響力的這個觀點。

grasp + significance 理解重要性

Most of my students are experienced enough that they quickly <u>grasp the significance of</u> honest communication.
大多數我的學生都有夠多的經驗，很快就能理解誠實溝通的重要性。

grasp + importance 理解重要性

The prime minister wanted the government to <u>grasp the importance of</u> global warming.
首相希望政府能夠意識到全球暖化的重要性。

grasp + meaning 理解含義

We have learned from our failures and <u>grasped the true meaning of</u> feedback to meet the needs of clients.
我們從失敗中學習，並理解回饋的真正用意，來滿足客戶的需求。

grasp + essence 理解本質

We must <u>grasp the essence of</u> things and should not just look at appearances.
我們必須掌握事物的本質，而不該只看表面而已。

grasp + basics 掌握基本知識

Our education system expects high school students to <u>grasp the basics of</u> science, technology, engineering and mathematics.
我們的教育體制期待高中生具備科學、科技、工程和數學的基本知識。

grasp + opportunity 把握機會

Let's <u>grasp the opportunity</u> that is presented by innovation to build a better future for the music industry.
讓我們把握創新所帶來的機會，為音樂產業創造更好的未來。

實用短語 / 用法 / 句型

1. grasp the nettle 積極處理困難、棘手問題

Even if the politicians <u>grasp the nettle</u>, the reforms are unlikely to come to fruition until 2032 at the earliest.

即使政治人物能處理棘手的問題，改革最快也要 2032 年才能看到效果。

2. grasp hold of sth 抓住、把握住～

If the party can <u>grasp hold of</u> the needed policy changes, chances are high that the party can be rebuilt.

如果該黨能夠把握必要的政策改革，那麼重建政黨的機會就很大。

Harm

▶ MP3-048

(harm — harmed — harmed)

harm + environment 危害環境

Protesters fear the nuclear facility will <u>harm the environment</u> and impact their livelihoods.
抗議者擔心核設施會危害環境並影響他們的生計。

harm + economy 損害經濟

Suspending visas for international students will ultimately <u>harm the</u> US <u>economy</u> because these students are vital to the country's creativity and competitiveness.
暫停發放簽證給國際學生最後將損害美國經濟，因為這些學生對於美國的創造力和競爭力至關重要。

harm + business 損害生意、業務

These additional costs of doing business, new limitations on advertising and changes to our business model could <u>harm our business</u>.
這些額外的營運成本、新的廣告限制以及商業模式的改變，都可能影響我們的業務。

harm + industry 損害產業

Rather than improving the financial system and protecting taxpayers, the reform will only <u>harm the industry</u> and stifle economic growth.

這項改革無法改善金融體系和保護納稅人，反而還會損害產業、抑制經濟成長。

harm + reputation 損害名聲

Although some cuts will certainly be necessary, major program reductions could <u>harm the</u> university's <u>reputation</u>.

雖然一些刪減是必要的，但刪減重大項目可能有損大學的名聲。

harm + eyes 傷害眼睛

While most people are aware of how harmful UV radiation is to the skin, many may not realize that UV radiation can also <u>harm the eyes</u>.

雖然大多數人都知道紫外線對皮膚的危害，但很多人可能沒有意識到紫外線也對眼睛有害。

Hinder

▶ MP3-049

(hinder — hindered — hindered)

hinder + development 阻礙發展

The results suggest that a high unemployment rate can <u>hinder the development of</u> democracy or threaten its existence.

結果顯示，高失業率會阻礙民主的發展或對其有所威脅。

hinder + progress 阻礙進展、進步

The public relations crisis could <u>hinder the progress</u> that we are hoping to make in these meetings next week.

公關危機可能會阻礙我們期望在下週會議上取得的進展。

hinder + growth 阻礙抑制成長

These policy changes could <u>hinder the growth of</u> the online advertising market, which could negatively impact Facebook.

這些政策上的改變可能會阻礙線上廣告市場的成長，且可能對 Facebook 產生負面影響。

hinder + performance 阻礙表現

We will discuss how characteristics may interact with employees' aptitudes and productivity, either to facilitate or to <u>hinder job performance</u>.

我們將討論人格特質是如何與員工資質和工作效率相互影響，進而提升或阻礙工作表現。

hinder + work 阻礙工作進行

The view that travel restrictions are unnecessary will directly <u>hinder the work</u> that needs to be undertaken to contain the virus.

認為旅行限制是不必要的這個觀點，將直接阻礙控制病毒所須進行的工作。

hinder + ability 阻礙能力

The global economic recession could <u>hinder the ability of</u> countries to take necessary steps to combat climate change.

全球經濟衰退可能會阻礙各國採取必要措施應對氣候變遷的能力。

hinder + recovery 阻礙復甦

The end result of such investment decisions will <u>hinder</u>, not help the US, <u>economic recovery</u>.

這類投資決策的結果可能會阻礙而不是幫助美國經濟復甦。

hinder + innovation 阻礙創新

The debate raging on today is whether patents promote or actually <u>hinder innovation</u>.
今天激烈的爭論圍繞在專利是促進、還是實際上阻礙了創新。

hinder + productivity 降低工作效率、生產力

Your phone can make you feel connected and less alone. However, because of that, it can also distract you from your work and <u>hinder productivity</u>.
手機可以讓你感覺與外界同在、不會那麼孤單。然而，正因為如此，它也會讓你無法專心工作、降低工作效率。

Hit

(hit — hit — hit)

hit + target 擊中目標

With this tracker, you are able to judge if your missile will successfully <u>hit the target</u> after launch.

有了這個追蹤器，你可以判斷飛彈在發射後是否會成功命中目標。

hit + peak 達到高峰

A lot of countries remain under lockdown and some experts fear that we could <u>hit a peak</u> in contagion in the second half of the year.

許多國家仍處於封城狀態，一些專家擔心，疫情可能會在今年下半年達到高峰。

hit + snag 碰到問題、困難

The global renewable energy market has recently <u>hit a snag</u> with falling prices.

全球再生能源市場最近遇到價格下跌的問題。

hit + problem 碰到問題、困難

If we keep sweeping global warming under the carpet, we are going to <u>hit major problems</u>.

如果我們繼續隱瞞全球暖化的事實，將會面臨嚴重的問題。

hit the market 上市

The new iPhone has just been unveiled and is expected to
<u>hit the market</u> on the 20th this month
新款 iPhone 剛剛發表，預計將於這個月 20 號上市。

hit the shelves 上市、上架

The iPhone 12 has <u>hit the shelves</u> worldwide, and Apple is
struggling to fill orders amid strong demand.
iPhone 12 已經在世界各地上市，在強勁的需求下，蘋果正努力出
貨。

hit the shops 上市

The sneaker will only be released in men's sizes and should
<u>hit the shops</u> at the end of July.
這款運動鞋只會推出男生尺寸，預計將於 7 月底上市。

hit the headlines 成為新聞頭條

The COVID-19 pandemic <u>hit the headlines</u> around the world
and many feared it could escalate into a global crisis.
COVID-19 傳染病成為世界各地的頭條新聞，許多人擔心它會升級
成全球性的危機。

hit the road 出發、上路

Let's <u>hit the road</u> as soon as possible so that we don't get
caught in traffic.
我們趕快出發以免塞車。

hit the streets 走上街頭

There is a massive upsurge in opposition to police brutality, and tens of thousands of people <u>hit the streets</u> all across the United States.
反對警察暴行的呼聲高漲，全美國有上萬人走上街頭。

hit the bed 上床睡覺

It's been a long day. We are going to go back to the hotel and <u>hit the bed</u>.
真是漫長的一天。我們準備要回飯店睡覺了。

hit the shower 沖個澡

I was going to head home to relax a little, but I definitely needed to <u>hit the shower</u> first.
我打算回家休息一下，但我絕對需要先沖個澡。

實用短語 / 用法 / 句型

1. hit the mark 達到目標；成功

Many analysts believe Google shares will <u>hit the</u> $700 <u>mark</u> within the next 12 months.
許多分析師認為，Google 的股價將在未來的 12 個月內攻上 700 美元大關。

2. hit the wall 遇到撞牆期（無法做出突破、進步）

To prevent businesses from <u>hitting the wall</u>, operators must ensure their financial management is strong and streamlined.

為了避免企業遇到撞牆期，經營者必須確保他們的財務管理是穩健而且有效率的。

3. hit rock bottom 跌到谷底；陷入低潮

Analysts say that the value of the US dollar could <u>hit rock bottom</u> in the next few months.

分析師說，美元的價值可能在未來幾個月內跌到谷底。

4. hit the spot 正好符合需求、正是某人要的

For a cold day, hot pot will be sure to <u>hit the spot</u>.

在寒冷的天氣裡，吃火鍋一定很適合。

5. hit the bottle 酗酒

The couple soon had a baby and lived a happy life, but everything changed when Charles began to <u>hit the bottle</u>.

這對夫妻很快就有了孩子，過著幸福的生活，但自從 Charles 開始酗酒，一切都變了。

6. hit the sack 上床睡覺

It's a big day tomorrow. We are going to have some dinner and <u>hit the sack</u> early.

明天是個大日子。我們打算吃個晚餐，然後早點睡覺。

A
B
C
D
E
F
G
H
I
J
K
L
M
N
O
P
Q
R
S
T
U
V
W

7. hit the panic button 驚慌失措、倉促行事

Don't <u>hit the panic button</u>. I'm sure we can solve
the problem with a little rational thought.
不要驚慌失措。我相信只要稍微理性思考一下，我們就能
解決這個問題。

8. hit the big time 成功、出名

As the actor began to <u>hit the big time</u>, his
relationship with his brother suffered.
當這位演員開始出名時，他和哥哥的關係受到了影響。

9. hit the nail on the head 一針見血、講到重點

I think you just <u>hit the nail on the head</u>. The point is
how companies create a healthy work environment
while trying to improve operational efficiency.
我覺得你講到重點了，關鍵是公司如何在努力提高營運效
率的同時，創造一個健康的工作環境。

10. hit home 戳到痛處（點醒某人讓他接受事實）

I came across a video online, which really <u>hit
home for</u> me, making me start to make some
changes in my life.
我在網路上看到一段影片，它深深戳到我的痛處，使我
開始改變生活。

Hold

▶ MP3-051

(hold — held — held)

---

hold + view 認為、抱持觀點

Competing for high-end foreign talent is a growing trend. Many universities <u>hold the view</u> that international students should be regarded as talent and not a threat to national security.

吸引頂尖人才是一個日益增長的趨勢。許多大學認為國際學生應該被視為人才，而不是對國家安全的威脅。

---

hold + position 擔任職位

After 27 years of being CEO of Amazon, Jeff Bezos will step aside and <u>hold the position of</u> executive president of the company's board of directors.

在擔任亞馬遜執行長 27 年之後，Jeff Bezos 即將卸任，轉為公司董事會執行董事長一職。

---

hold + office 擔任職位、執政

Whoever wins the election tonight will <u>hold office</u> for four years and lead the country forward.

在今晚選舉中勝出的人將會執政 4 年，帶領國家向前發展。

hold + record 保持紀錄

A former Los Angeles Lakers superstar, Wilt Chamberlain, still <u>holds the all-time</u> NBA <u>record</u> which even Michael Jordan and the late Kobe Bryant have never exceeded.
前洛杉磯湖人隊的超級球星 Wilt Chamberlain 至今仍保持 NBA 的歷史紀錄，甚至 Michael Jordan 和已故球星 Kobe Bryant 也從未超越。

hold + lead 保持領先

While Pfizer and Moderna <u>hold the lead</u>, new data from J&J and Novavax show there is room for everyone in the vaccine market.
雖然輝瑞和莫德納在疫苗市場保有領先地位，但嬌生和諾瓦瓦克斯的最新數據顯示，在疫苗市場上，每個品牌都有發展空間。

hold + promise 抱有希望

The results <u>hold promise for</u> eventual clinical applications that may spur brain repair after stroke.
該研究結果有望用於刺激中風後腦部修復的臨床應用。

hold + attention 吸引注意力

Since the young are easily distracted, a keynote speaker's ability to <u>hold their attention</u> is particularly important.
由於年輕人很容易分心，簡報講者吸引他們注意的能力就顯得特別重要。

hold + interest 抱有興趣

I guess, for the most part, the news will <u>hold little interest for</u> her.
我想她對這個消息多半不會有興趣。

hold + grudge 懷恨在心、怨恨

When we <u>hold a grudge against</u> someone, even a trivial thing can fuel a conflict.
當我們對某人懷恨在心，即使是很小的事情也可能引發衝突。

hold + meeting 開會

As many companies convert their office space to open-plan offices, huddle rooms offer a place where employees can <u>hold meetings</u> without disturbing colleagues.
由於很多公司都將辦公空間改造成開放式辦公室，小型會議空間提供了一個可以開會，而不會打擾同事的地方。

hold + conference 舉行會議

The administration <u>held a press conference</u> and allowed reporters to ask anything they would like.
政府召開了記者會，讓記者提出任何想問的問題。

hold + election 舉行選舉

The question remains whether or not we should <u>hold elections</u> in the midst of a pandemic.
問題仍然是，我們是否應該在疫情期間舉行選舉。

hold + talks 進行會談

The Ministry of Foreign Affairs on Monday confirmed that it had <u>held talks with</u> members of the US Congress <u>on</u> changing the name of its office in Washington, D.C.

外交部週一證實,已經與美國國會議員針對更改華盛頓特區辦事處名稱一事進行了會談。

hold + conversation 進行對話、交談

To be able to <u>hold a good conversation with</u> your team, you should first listen to them for a couple of minutes, instead of projecting your ideas onto them.

為了能夠與團隊進行良好的溝通,你應該先聽他們講個幾分鐘,而不是將你的想法投射在他們身上。

實用短語 / 用法 / 句型

1. hold the key 掌握關鍵

The result of that experiment might <u>hold the key to</u> unlocking the secrets of cancer.

這個實驗結果可能掌握了解開癌症祕密的關鍵。

Illustrate

▶ MP3-052

(illustrate — illustrated — illustrated)

illustrate + point 說明觀點

<u>To illustrate the point</u>, she showed the statistics that roughly one in five rural schools are reportedly on the brink of closure.

為了説明這一點，她提出了一項統計數據，指出大約五分之一的偏鄉學校瀕臨廢校。

illustrate + difference 說明差異

I merely make these points to <u>illustrate the difference between</u> teaching universities and research universities.

我講這些只是為了説明教學型大學和研究型大學的差異。

illustrate + importance 說明重要性

These two patients' very different outcomes starkly <u>illustrate the importance of</u> early diagnosis and treatment.

這兩名患者截然不同的結果，清楚説明了及早診斷與治療的重要性。

Implement

(implement — implemented — implemented)

implement + plan 實行計畫

We have an ambitious plan for the subway system, but there is one catch. We don't have enough funding to <u>implement the plan</u>.

針對地鐵系統，我們有一個遠大的計畫，但是有個問題，我們沒有足夠的資金來實行這個計畫。

implement + program 實行計畫

The COVID-19 Prevention <u>Program</u> will <u>be implemented</u> on December 1, and travelers must provide a COVID-19 nucleic acid test report issued within three days prior to boarding a flight to Taiwan.

12 月 1 日起實施 COVID-19 疫情防治計畫，旅客須提供登機前 3 日內的核酸檢驗報告。

implement + policy 實施政策、策略

To get the best results, you can follow the steps and <u>implement these policies</u>.

為了獲得最佳結果，你可以按照以下步驟實施這些策略。

implement + decision 實行決策

Under these circumstances, this will be one of the ways that we can support our school staff as we <u>implement the decision</u> to reopen schools.

在這種情況下，當我們實施重啟校園的決策時，這會是我們可以支持學校職員的方式之一。

implement + measures 實施措施

The jump has raised concern that the property market may overheat, leading the government to <u>implement measures</u> to cool the market.

房價飆漲引發了人們對房地產市場可能過熱的擔憂，促使政府採取措施讓市場降溫。

implement + recommendations 實行建議

The government should support the National Health Insurance Administration to <u>implement the recommendations</u> to ensure that all necessary improvements are delivered for the benefit of patients.

政府應支持健保署實行這些建議，以確保所有必要的改善措施都能造福病患。

A
B
C
D
E
F
G
H
I
J
K
L
M
N
O
P
Q
R
S
T
U
V
W

implement + strategy 實施策略

The manager's apparent hesitation to <u>implement the strategy</u> he announced in March leaves many analysts confused.

經理對於執行他在 3 月宣布的策略明顯猶豫不決，這讓許多分析師感到困惑。

implement + changes 執行、進行改變

On the basis of customer research, we have to refine overall user experience, and then work with the digital marketing team to <u>implement changes</u>.

基於顧客調查，我們必須優化整體的使用者體驗，並與數位行銷團隊合作來進行改變。

implement + requirements 實施規定、要求

After the bill is passed, schools will have a transition period of at least one full school year to <u>implement the</u> new <u>requirements</u>.

法案通過後，學校將有至少一個學年的過渡期來實施新規定。

Impede

▶ MP3-054

(impede — impeded — impeded)

impede + progress 阻礙進展、進步

Though it's still too early to tell what impact it may have overall, a lack of advertising agencies could potentially impede the project's progress.

雖然現在說會產生什麼影響還太早，但缺少廣告代理商可能會阻礙這個企劃的進展。

impede + development 阻礙發展

Australia is home to some of the world's top stem cell researchers, and advocates argue that if the bill is vetoed, this will seriously impede the development of stem cell therapy.

澳洲有一些世界頂尖的幹細胞研究人員，支持者認為如果該法案被否決，這將嚴重阻礙幹細胞治療的發展。

impede + growth 阻礙成長、增長

There is no chance these countries will be willing to impede economic growth in the name of clean energy.

這些國家不可能願意為了綠能而阻礙經濟發展。

A
B
C
D
E
F
G
H
I
J
K
L
M
N
O
P
Q
R
S
T
U
V
W

impede + ability 阻礙能力

We have repeatedly called on authorities to unblock media websites, eliminate restrictions that <u>impede the ability of</u> journalists to practice their profession, and allow all individuals to express their views without fear of retribution.
我們已多次呼籲政府解除對媒體網站的封鎖、取消妨礙記者從事其專業的限制，並允許所有人發表自己的觀點，而不必擔心遭受報復。

impede + access 阻礙取得的機會

Societal attitudes towards people with disabilities continue to <u>impede their access to</u> jobs in private sectors.
社會大眾對身心障礙者的態度，持續阻礙他們在私人企業取得工作。

impede + communication 阻礙溝通

Our research has shown there are barriers to collaboration. For example, different professions, educational backgrounds, and different first languages can <u>impede</u> effective <u>communication</u>.
我們的研究顯示，合作上有些阻礙，例如不同的職業、教育背景和不同的母語，可能都會妨礙有效溝通。

impede + efforts 阻礙努力

The political gridlock has undermined public confidence and <u>impeded our efforts to</u> take the steps we need for our economy.

政治僵局打擊了民眾的信心，阻礙我們為經濟發展採取必要措施的努力。

impede + recovery 阻礙恢復

The infections and other complications can <u>impede</u> patients' <u>recovery from</u> cardiac surgery.

感染以及其他併發症可能阻礙患者心臟手術後的復原。

Impose

(impose — imposed — imposed)

impose + sanctions 實施制裁

This new law will <u>impose sanctions on</u> foreign companies that do business in Iran's energy sector.
這項新法律將對在伊朗能源產業做生意的外國公司實施制裁。

impose + restrictions 限制、約束

Public outrage has prompted the government to <u>impose restrictions on</u> the use of force against civilians by police officers.
民眾的憤怒促使政府限制警察對市民使用武力。

impose + conditions 施加條件

Countries that extend financial help have a right to <u>impose conditions</u> to ensure that their loans are repaid.
提供財政援助的國家有權施加條件，以確保借出去的錢能拿得回來。

impose + limits 限制

Clubhouse <u>imposes limits on</u> the number of people that can participate in a conversation at any time.
Clubhouse 限制了同時可以進入房間參與對話的人數。

impose + ban 禁止

Taiwan is the second Asian country to <u>impose a ban on</u> smoking in all enclosed public places including bars and restaurants.
臺灣是第二個禁止在任何密閉的公共場所吸菸的亞洲國家，這些場所包含酒吧和餐廳在內。

impose + taxes 課稅

The news that the administration is planning to <u>impose taxes on</u> capital gains has provoked a backlash from investors.
政府計劃課徵資本利得稅的消息引起了投資人的強烈反對。

impose + fines 開罰、處以罰鍰

Several countries are <u>imposing fines on</u> people for spreading misinformation about the coronavirus pandemic.
有些國家正在對散布新冠肺炎疫情假消息的人開罰。

impose + burden 帶來負擔

The enormous expense of public healthcare will <u>impose</u> another <u>heavy burden on</u> our shaky economy.
龐大的公共醫療保健支出，將為我們搖搖欲墜的經濟帶來另一個沉重的負擔。

Improve

▶ MP3-056

(improve — improved — improved)

improve + quality 提升品質

Artificial intelligence has the potential to <u>improve the quality of</u> life but may also cause harm.
人工智慧有可能提高生活品質，但也可能造成危害。

improve + performance 改善表現、提升表現

There is no reason why we shouldn't apply the knowledge we have acquired in learning science to <u>improve</u> student <u>performance</u>.
我們沒有理由不應用我們在學習科學中所學到的知識，來提升學生的表現。

improve + efficiency 提高效率

Now it appears that we are entering a new stage of development—artificial intelligence is <u>improving operational efficiency</u>, and self-driving cars are improving our safety.
看起來我們正進入一個新的發展階段：人工智慧正在提高營運效率，自動駕駛汽車正在提升我們的安全性。

improve + productivity 提高生產力

To increase profits, we need to continually look to <u>improve productivity</u> and reduce costs where possible.
為了增加利潤，我們需要不斷提高產能，也要盡可能降低成本。

improve + situation 改善情況

It is not impossible for you to <u>improve the situation</u>, but it will be difficult.
對你來說，要改善這種情況不是不可能，但很困難。

improve + conditions 改善條件（特別指生活條件、工作條件）

Uber asserts that it recognizes the need to <u>improve conditions for</u> its drivers, but it depends on regulatory change to realize that goal.
Uber 聲稱有必要改善司機的工作條件，但要實現這個目標，還需要制度上的改革。

improve + service 提升服務

We help our clients use technology to increase profits, <u>improve service</u>, and differentiate themselves from competitors.
我們幫助客戶利用科技來增加利潤、提升服務品質，並做出與競爭對手的差異。

improve + health 增進健康

According to a report by the World Health Organization, good nutrition can help <u>improve health</u> and lower the risk of disease at all ages.
根據世界衛生組織的報告顯示，良好的營養可以幫助各年齡層的人改善健康並降低疾病風險。

Increase

▶ MP3-057

(increase — increased — increased)

increase + number 增加數量（後面接可數名詞）

The city plans to <u>increase the number of</u> public housing units as a way to lower housing prices.
該城市計劃增加社會住宅的數量來降低房價。

increase + amount 增加數量（後面接不可數名詞）

When YouTube suggests videos, they prefer those that <u>increase the amount of</u> time that the viewer will spend on the platform.
當 YouTube 在推薦影片時，他們更喜歡推薦那些能增加觀眾在平台上觀看時間的影片。

increase + likelihood 增加可能性

Climate change may <u>increase the likelihood of</u> floods, hurricanes, blizzards, and the resulting destruction.
氣候變遷可能會增加發生水災、颶風、暴風雪以及隨之而來的災害的可能性。

increase + probability 增加可能性

The paper shows that even small increases in global temperatures can significantly <u>increase the probability of</u> extreme weather events, particularly heat waves and heavy rainfall.

這篇論文指出，即使全球氣溫稍稍上升，也會大幅增加極端氣候事件發生的可能性，尤其像是熱浪和暴雨。

increase + chance 增加機會

Diversifying your portfolio will <u>increase the chances of</u> beating the market and getting good returns, especially in the case of a market crash.

特別是在市場崩跌的情況下，分散投資組合將增加你打贏大盤、獲得高報酬的機會。

increase + risk 增加風險

Non-essential travel is not recommended because it <u>increases the risk of</u> contracting and spreading COVID-19.

不建議從事非必要的旅遊，因為會增加感染和傳播 COVID-19 的風險。

increase + cost 增加成本

When consumer prices rise, it <u>increases the cost of</u> living for the average family.

當消費者物價上漲時，它增加了一般家庭的生活成本。

increase + value 增加價值

We need to figure out how to <u>increase the value of</u> our products and services instead of offering giveaways to consumers.

我們需要找出如何增加產品和服務的價值，而不是提供贈品給消費者。

increase + awareness 提高意識

The Breast Cancer Foundation is aimed at further <u>increasing the awareness of</u> breast cancer among female university students.

這個乳癌防治基金會旨在進一步提高女大學生對乳癌的認識。

increase + efficiency 提高效率

By turning on Do Not Disturb or Airplane mode on your phone, you can focus more on the task at hand and vastly <u>increase efficiency</u>.

打開手機的勿擾或是飛航模式，你可以更專注在手邊的事情，並且能大大地提高效率。

increase + productivity 提高生產力

One way to <u>increase productivity</u> at work is to avoid scheduling events that don't accomplish much, like routine meetings.

提高工作效率的一個方法是，避免安排一些沒什麼作用的事情，像是例行會議。

increase + sales 提高銷售量

No matter how big your company is, focusing on growing a loyal customer base can help <u>increase sales</u> and accelerate the growth of your business.

無論你的公司多大，專注於發展忠實的客戶群，都可以幫助提高銷售額並加速業務成長。

Induce

▶ MP3-058

(induce — induced — induced)

induce + vomiting 催吐、引發嘔吐

If your child swallows hand sanitizer, don't try to <u>induce vomiting</u> because it can make things worse.
如果您的孩子誤食乾洗手,請勿嘗試催吐,因為這會使情況變得更糟。

induce + sleep 促進睡眠

Taking a warm bath and reading a book will help relax your body and <u>induce sleep</u>.
洗個熱水澡、看看書,會幫助你放鬆身體、促進睡眠。

induce + changes 引起變化

The education sector continues to feel the impact of pandemic-<u>induced changes</u> such as delayed exams and deferred admission.
疫情造成的改變持續影響教育界,例如考試延期以及延後入學。

Influence

▶ MP3-059

(influence — influenced — influenced)

influence + outcome 影響結果

The pension reform will <u>influence the outcome of</u> the next presidential election—which takes place in 2024.
年金改革將影響下一屆 2024 總統大選的結果。

influence + development 影響發展

Studies provide evidence that children's early pain experience can <u>influence the development of</u> their nervous system.
研究提供的證據顯示，兒童早期的疼痛經驗可能會影響其神經系統的發育。

influence + way 影響～的方式

We are seeing how closely social media is starting to <u>influence the way</u> we think.
我們正看到社群媒體開始密切影響我們的思維方式。

influence + decision 影響決定

I don't want to <u>influence the decision</u> because as a host I'm not really allowed, but I have to say we share the same view.
我不想影響這個決定，因為作為一名主持人，我不能這樣做，但不得不說，我們的觀點是一致的。

influence + choice 影響選擇

What are the factors that might <u>influence the choice of</u> marketing strategies across different situations?
在不同的情況下，有哪些因素可能會影響行銷策略的選擇？

influence + opinion 影響看法

Newspaper headlines can <u>influence public opinion</u>, which may, in turn, impact policy decisions.
報紙標題會影響公眾輿論，可能進而影響政策決定。

influence + behavior 影響行為

There has been heated debate about whether violent video games <u>influence</u> children's <u>behavior</u>.
關於暴力電玩是否會影響兒童的行為，一直存在著激烈的爭論。

Interrupt

▶ MP3-060

(interrupt — interrupted — interrupted)

interrupt + flow　打斷節奏

Tribal members actually do not want infrastructure and they don't want to <u>interrupt the flow of</u> life in the environment.
部落成員實際上不想要基礎設施，也不希望打亂環境中生物的生活。

interrupt + process　中斷過程

A higher rate of inflation could <u>interrupt the process of</u> economic recovery by darkening the investment outlook.
較高的通貨膨脹率使投資前景變得黯淡，可能進而打斷經濟復甦的過程。

interrupt + service　中斷服務

If you live in one of the heavily connected places like Taiwan, it is very unlikely that a natural disaster is going to <u>interrupt</u> your Internet <u>service</u>.
如果你生活在像臺灣這樣網路高度密集的地方，單一的天然災害不太可能會中斷你的網路服務。

Invade

▶ MP3-061

(invade — invaded — invaded)

invade + privacy 侵犯隱私

The concern is that companies will use the technology to <u>invade the privacy of</u> workers and use it as a way to keep them in line.

令人擔憂的是，公司將利用這項技術來侵犯員工的隱私，並以此作為讓他們遵守規定的方式。

invade + rights 侵犯權利

We don't want to <u>invade the rights of</u> those who don't smoke, and to do that we need more smoking rooms in public areas.

我們不想侵犯那些沒有抽菸的人的權利，為了做到這一點，我們需要在公共場所增設更多的吸菸室。

invade + country 入侵國家

More than 4 million refugees have fled Ukraine since Russia <u>invaded the country</u> in late February.

自 2 月下旬俄羅斯入侵烏克蘭以來，已經有超過 400 萬難民逃離烏克蘭。

invade + territory 入侵領土、領域

Digital technology is changing the financial industry as fintech startups <u>invade the territory of</u> closely-regulated traditional lenders.

隨著金融科技新創搶攻受到嚴格監管的傳統銀行地盤，數位科技正在改變金融業。

Irritate

▶ MP3-062

(irritate — irritated — irritated)

irritate + skin 刺激皮膚

The lotion uses no animal fats or chemicals that can <u>irritate the skin</u>.
這款乳液沒有使用任何會刺激皮膚的動物性脂肪或化學物質。

irritate + eyes 刺激眼睛

The gas is known to slowly release into the air and can <u>irritate eyes</u> and cause breathing problems.
這種氣體會慢慢地擴散到空氣中，而且會刺激眼睛並造成呼吸問題。

irritate + stomach 刺激胃

Some medications should be taken with or immediately after a meal to reduce the risk of <u>irritating the stomach</u>.
有些藥物應該隨餐服用或於餐後立即服用，以減少刺激胃部的風險。

Jeopardize

▶ MP3-063

(jeopardize — jeopardized — jeopardized)

jeopardize + safety 危及安全

The officer turned those offers down, and made it clear that he would never reveal any secrets that could <u>jeopardize the safety of</u> his fellows.

軍官拒絕了這些提議，並明確表示他永遠不會洩露任何可能危及同伴安全的祕密。

jeopardize + security 危及安全

The foreign affairs analyst said that military action by China against Taiwan could <u>jeopardize the security of</u> Japan.

國際事務分析師説，中國對臺灣的軍事行動可能危及日本的安全。

jeopardize + health 危害健康

You might not want to <u>jeopardize the health of</u> your friends and family simply because it is inconvenient to wear a mask.

你可能不想僅僅因為戴口罩的不便，而危害到朋友和家人的健康。

jeopardize + success 危及成功

There have been concerns that public distrust of the vaccines could <u>jeopardize the success of</u> vaccination programs.

有人擔心民眾對疫苗的不信任，可能危及疫苗接種計畫能否成功。

jeopardize + future 危及、影響未來

Although machine automation makes our daily lives easier, robots could <u>jeopardize the future of</u> employment in restaurants.

儘管機械自動化使我們的日常生活變得更方便，但是機器人可能會危及未來餐廳的就業情況。

Justify

▶ MP3-064

(justify — justified — justified)

justify + use 證明～使用的正當性、合理化～的使用

The administration appears to have increasingly abused emergency authority to <u>justify the use of</u> force against citizens exercising their right to assemble peacefully.
政府似乎越來越濫用緊急權力，來證明對行使和平集會權的公民使用武力是正當的。

justify + means 證明方法、手段是合理的

If thousands of users visit your website but do nothing, you are sure that heavy traffic does not <u>justify the means of</u> marketing.
如果有數千名用戶瀏覽你的網站，但卻沒有任何動作，那麼你可以確定，高流量並無法證明行銷方法是對的。

justify + cost 證明費用是合理的

Maybe that strategy would work, but the benefits it brings would not be great enough to <u>justify the</u> huge <u>cost</u>.
或許這個策略可行，但帶來的好處還不足以證明它的鉅額費用是合理的。

A
B
C
D
E
F
G
H
I
J
K
L
M
N
O
P
Q
R
S
T
U
V
W

justify + expense 證明花費是合理的

Routine or short-distance business travel probably doesn't justify the expense of travel insurance.
例行性或短途的商務旅行可能不值得購買旅行保險。

justify + action 合理化舉動

Whenever we take an action, we usually create a story to justify the action and we are not aware that we are doing it.
每當我們採取行動時，我們通常會編一個故事來證明我們的行動是合理的，而我們並沒有意識到自己正在這麼做。

justify + conclusion 證明結論是合理的

There is no direct evidence to justify the conclusion that the vaccine can cause serious reactions.
沒有直接證據可以證明疫苗會引起嚴重反應的結論是合理的。

justify + purchase 證明購買的合理性

The publicly traded company is trying to figure out how to justify the purchase of property to investors.
這家上市公司試著想要如何向投資人證明購買土地的合理性。

justify + need 證明必要性、需求

The reports were written to justify the need to spend billions of New Taiwan dollars (NTD) on building a new plant.
這些報告是為了證明花費數十億新臺幣來建造新廠房的必要性。

justify + investment 證明投資是合理的

The greater the risk a businessman assumes, the greater the anticipated profit needed to <u>justify the investment</u>.
商人承受的風險越高，就需要越高的預期利潤來證明這項投資是合理的。

Kick

(kick — kicked — kicked)

kick + habit 改掉習慣

As a heavy smoker, I've tried to <u>kick the habit</u>, but it didn't quite work out the way I hoped it would.
身為癮君子，我嘗試改掉抽菸的習慣，但結果並不如預期。

實用短語 / 用法 / 句型

1. kick the tires 在購買之前仔細檢查、試用

You should always <u>kick the tires of</u> any equipment you plan to buy, or you might end up buying a piece of junk.
對於任何你打算購買的設備，在購買前都應該仔細檢查，否則你可能會買到垃圾。

2. kick the bucket 死掉

We all have a to-do list of things to accomplish before we get old or <u>kick the bucket</u>.
在我們變老或死掉之前，我們都有一些代辦清單上的事情想完成。

3. kick up one's heels 好好享受、盡情享樂

Taiwanese people <u>kick up their heels</u> on this holiday in many ways, but most people have barbecues.
臺灣人在這個節日有很多慶祝方式，但大多數的人都會烤肉。

Knock

▶ MP3-066

(knock — knocked — knocked)

knock on the door 敲門

Some have the custom of <u>knocking on the door</u> before entering, as a sign of politeness.
有些人習慣進門前先敲門，以示禮貌。

knock sb unconscious 把某人打昏

Her mother <u>was knocked unconscious</u> in the 7.0-magnitude earthquake and taken to a hospital.
她母親在規模 7.0 的地震中被砸中、失去意識，而被送往醫院。

knock down the price 降價；殺價

Overall, the car is just in fair condition. It is on the edge of what I would purchase, but I think these problems will help me <u>knock down the price</u>.
整體來說，這輛車的狀況還可以，算是符合我想要購買的條件，但我認為這些問題可以幫我降低買價。

實用短語 / 用法 / 句型

1. knock on wood 別烏鴉嘴、呸呸呸（祈求壞事不要發生）

I had close contact with someone with COVID-19, but I've tested negative and have had no symptoms so far. Knock on wood.

雖然我和 COVID-19 確診者有過密切接觸，但我目前檢測陰性而且沒有任何症狀。呸呸呸，希望不要確診。

2. knock one's socks off 令人震驚、驚艷

All mobile carriers believe that 5G, the network coming after 4G, will be so fast that it is going to knock your socks off.

所有的行動電信業者都認為，繼 4G 之後的 5G 網路，速度將會快到讓人驚艷。

3. knock it off 停止、住口

My suggestion to both of you is to knock it off, and keep your thoughts to yourself.

我給你們的建議是都先別說了，把你們的想法留在心裡就好。

Lay
(lay — laid — laid)

▶ MP3-067

lay + bet 打賭

It's likely I'm terrible at betting this season. I feel like I lose every time I <u>lay a bet on</u> the Brothers and the Uni-Lions.
這個賽季我的賭運很差,感覺每次押兄弟象和統一獅都會輸。

lay + wager 打賭

If I were a betting man, I'd <u>lay a wager</u> that we can expect to see the launch of something that offers a health monitoring service.
如果讓我來賭,我敢打賭我們可以期待看到提供健康監測服務的產品推出。

lay + foundation 奠定基礎

We will act not only to create new jobs, but to <u>lay a</u> new <u>foundation for</u> future growth.
我們將採取行動,不只是為了創造新的工作機會,也是為了未來的發展奠定新的基礎。

lay + blame 指責、咎責

Unfortunately, there are too many people out there that <u>lay blame on</u> the parents.
不幸的是,太多人把責任推到父母身上。

lay + charge 控告某人

The government is planning to <u>lay a charge against</u> people spreading fake news about COVID-19.
政府打算對散播 COVID-19 假新聞的民眾提告。

lay + emphasis 強調、重視

When accounting for these results, I would like to <u>lay particular emphasis on</u> the fact that millennials are often more willing to pay for music streaming.
在解釋這些結果時，我想特別強調一點：千禧世代通常更願意付錢給串流音樂服務。

lay + stress 強調、重視

Doctors <u>lay great stress on</u> the need to conduct an annual physical exam and assess risk after a certain age.
醫生特別強調，到了一定的年紀之後，需要每年做健康檢查、評估風險。

實用短語 / 用法 / 句型

1. lay a hand / finger on sb 對某人動手、傷害某人
If you ever <u>lay a finger on</u> the children again, I will divorce you!
如果你敢再對孩子動手，我就跟你離婚！

2. lay hands on sth 得到、把～弄到手

I need to go to the library and <u>lay my hands on</u> this book for my research paper.
我需要去圖書館借這本書來寫論文。

3. lay claim to sth 宣稱～為自己所有

China and Japan have historically <u>laid claim to</u> the islands, which lie between the two nations.
中國和日本在歷史上都曾宣稱，對這些位於兩國之間的島嶼擁有主權。

4. lay it on the line 把話說清楚、明確說明

If you <u>lay it on the line</u>, maybe then they'll be able to understand how serious this situation is.
如果你把話說清楚，或許他們就能明白這狀況有多嚴重。

Lead

(lead — led — led)

lead + discussion 帶領、引導討論

Award-winning director Chloé Zhao will <u>lead a discussion</u> following the movie.
獲獎導演趙怡將在電影結束後帶領討論。

lead + team 帶領團隊

As a project manager, you are expected to help <u>lead the team</u> and make decisions based on your team's feedback.
身為專案經理，你應該領導團隊，並根據團隊的回饋做決定。

lead + country 帶領國家

They think this presidential candidate is better suited to <u>lead the country</u> through the financial crisis.
他們認為，這位總統候選人更適合帶領國家度過這次的金融危機。

lead + investigation 主導調查

In the early 2000s, the attorney <u>led the investigation of</u> the presidential election in Florida and negotiated human rights issues with the Chinese government.
在 2000 年代初期，這位律師主導調查佛羅里達州的總統大選結果，以及與中國政府協調人權問題。

lead + way 帶路

Before your trip, make sure you have an experienced mountaineer or a professional guide to <u>lead the way</u> to prevent accidents.
出發前，要確保有一位經驗豐富的登山者或是專業嚮導帶路，以免發生意外。

lead + life 過生活

Doctors told her that she wouldn't <u>lead a normal life</u> ever again and probably have to rely on a wheelchair for the rest of her life.
醫生告訴她，她將無法再過正常生活，可能下半輩子都必須仰賴輪椅。

實用短語 / 用法 / 句型

1. lead sb by the nose 牽著某人的鼻子走

Instead of <u>being led by the nose</u> by China, Australia should strengthen its local economy and communications with other countries in the Asia-Pacific region.
澳洲不應該被中國牽著鼻子走，而應該加強國內經濟以及與亞太地區其他國家的交流。

2. lead the world / market / pack / field 在世界 / 市場 /
群體 / 領域上居於領先

This investment will bolster our economy, attract
innovative talent, and help us continue to <u>lead the
world in</u> automobile manufacturing.
這項投資將振興我們的經濟、吸引創新人才,並幫助我們
在汽車製造業中保持世界領先地位。

3. lead the way in sth 在～處於領先地位、在～作為領
頭羊

High-tech industries will <u>lead the way in</u> driving
global economic recovery and building a post-
pandemic world.
高科技產業將作為全球經濟復甦的領頭羊,建構疫情後的
世界。

4. lead the eye 引導視線、注意力

Photography, like art, is subjective, but he stressed
how images should <u>lead the eye</u> and hold the
attention.
攝影就像藝術,是主觀的,但他強調影像應該如何引導視
線、吸引注意力。

Leave

▶ MP3-069

(leave — left — left)

---

leave + impression 留下印象

His contributions to our community <u>leave a lasting impression on</u> us. He will be dearly missed.
他對我們社區的貢獻讓我們留下深刻的印象，大家會非常想念他。

---

leave + message 留言、留訊息

If you have specific questions, please <u>leave a message</u>. Our team members will respond within three days.
如果你有特定的問題，歡迎留言。我們的團隊將在 3 天內回覆。

---

leave + note 留下字條

The man did not <u>leave a note</u> at the scene, but authorities have ruled out the possibility of foul play.
這名男子沒有在現場留下任何字條，但有關當局已經排除了他殺的可能。

---

leave + comment 留言、留下評論

If this video resonates with you, <u>leave a comment</u> down below and let me know how you like it.
如果這支影片引起你的共鳴，在下面留言告訴我你的想法。

leave + response 留下回應

If a story speaks to you, you can <u>leave a response</u> for the author and other readers to see.
如果故事很吸引你，你可以留言給作者或是其他讀者。

leave + tip 留下小費

In some countries, when we fail to <u>leave a tip</u>, it implies that we are less than happy with our meal.
在某些國家，如果我們沒有給小費，意味著我們對這頓飯不太滿意。

實用短語 / 用法 / 句型

1. leave a lot / much to be desired 還有很大的改進空間
The film has a very interesting premise and a story that has quite a bit of potential, but the final product <u>leaves a lot to be desired</u>.
這部電影有個很有趣的前情提要和劇情，相當有發展潛力，但最終的成品卻有很大的改進空間。

2. leave something / nothing to be desired 有待改進 / 無可挑剔
After viewing a number of apartments, unfortunately, I found that the layouts often <u>leave something to be desired</u>, even in the expensive ones.
可惜的是，看了幾間公寓之後，就算是那些比較貴的，我發現它們的格局都還是有待改進。

3. leave a bad taste in one's mouth 讓某人留下不好的印象

The way they conducted the interview <u>left a bad taste in my mouth</u>. I don't think I'd accept the job even if they offer it.
他們面試進行的方式讓我留下不好的印象，就算他們給我這份工作，我想我也不會接受。

Lift

(lift — lifted — lifted)

lift + spirits 提振精神、心情

American consumer confidence rebounded sharply in April, as the announcements about the vaccine trials <u>lifted</u> the nation's <u>spirits</u>.

疫苗試驗的公布提振了美國國內士氣，美國消費者信心在 4 月也隨之急遽反彈。

lift + mood 提振心情

Any pleasant home fragrance can act as a distraction and <u>lift mood</u>, but recent studies suggest that sweet smells may work best.

任何令人愉悅的室內擴香都可以分散注意力並提振心情，但最近的研究顯示，香甜的味道可能效果最好。

lift + ban 解除禁令、限制

The government plans to <u>lift the ban on</u> mask exports on June 1, meaning that local mask manufacturers are allowed to sell masks freely across markets.

政府計劃在 6 月 1 日解除口罩出口禁令，意味著當地口罩廠商可以在國內外市場自由銷售口罩。

lift + restriction 取消限制

The city is appealing to the government to <u>lift the restriction on</u> non-essential travel and help local businesses that have been severely affected.
該市呼籲政府取消非必要旅行的限制,並幫助受到嚴重影響的當地企業。

lift + sanctions 撤銷制裁

People are asking questions about why we would <u>lift sanctions</u> now, given that the regime is causing problems in other parts of the world.
人們在問,既然這個政權正在世界其他地區製造麻煩,我們為什麼要現在取消制裁。

lift + economy 提振經濟

The rise of a new economic power can help <u>lift the</u> entire global <u>economy</u>.
一個新經濟體的崛起可以幫助提振全球經濟。

實用短語 / 用法 / 句型

1. lift the lid 揭露真相

The film is about a young police officer and his struggle to <u>lift the lid on</u> corruption in the force.
這部電影講述的是一名年輕警官,他為揭露警隊的腐敗問題而奮鬥。

2. not lift a finger 不肯幫一點忙

It is outrageous that so many elected officials feign concern and compassion for these kids, but in fact they do <u>not lift a finger to</u> help them.

令人氣憤的是，許多民選官員假裝關心和同情這些孩子，但其實一點忙都不肯幫。

Lighten

▶ MP3-071

(lighten — lightened — lightened)

lighten + burden　減輕負擔

The government is hoping to use the Olympics to encourage people to work from home to <u>lighten the burden of</u> public transport.
政府希望藉由奧運來鼓勵民眾在家工作，減少公共運輸的負擔。

lighten + load　減輕負擔

I'm so sorry for your loss. If there's anything we can do to <u>lighten your load</u>, please don't hesitate to ask.
對你失去親人我感到很遺憾，如果我們可以做些什麼來減輕你的負擔，請儘管開口。

lighten + mood　使心情變好

Your sense of humor will actually help you build good relationships. People will want to work with you because you <u>lighten the mood</u> and take the pressure off.
你的幽默感會幫助你建立良好的人際關係，人們會願意和你一起工作，因為你使他們的心情變好、減輕了壓力。

lighten + atmosphere 緩和氣氛

Some teachers, male and female, use harmless jokes or mild sarcasm to <u>lighten the atmosphere</u> in a classroom.
有些老師，無論男女，會用無傷大雅的笑話或反諷來緩和課堂氣氛。

lighten + tone 緩和氣氛

I didn't mean to be disrespectful—I was just trying to <u>lighten the tone of</u> the meeting.
我不是有意冒犯，我只是想讓會議的氣氛輕鬆一點。

Lodge

▶ MP3-072

(lodge — lodged — lodged)

lodge + complaint 投訴

If you're not happy with the airline's policy, you can contact the Consumer Protection Committee and <u>lodge a complaint</u>.
如果你對航空公司的政策不滿意，你可以向消保會投訴。

lodge + claim 提出索賠

Strictly speaking, you must <u>lodge a</u> chargeback <u>claim with</u> your bank within 120 days of realizing that there is a problem.
嚴格來說，你必須在發現問題的 120 天內，向你的銀行提出退款要求。

lodge + protest 提出抗議

The government should <u>lodge a strong protest with</u> the Japanese government to defend the nation's food safety and the rights and interests of the nation's fishermen.
政府應該向日本政府提出嚴正抗議，以維護國家的食品安全和漁民權益。

lodge + appeal 提出上訴

She has <u>lodged an appeal with</u> the country's supreme court, but so far it has shown little interest.
她已經向國家最高法院提出上訴，但到目前為止，最高法院仍對此案不太在意。

Lower

(lower — lowered — lowered)

lower + cost 降低成本、費用

The policy seeks to expand insurance coverage and <u>lower the cost of</u> healthcare.
該政策的目的是擴大保險涵蓋範圍，並降低醫療保健的費用。

lower + price 降低價格

We can probably <u>lower the price</u> by 10% if you can commit to a large order.
如果你能答應大量訂貨，我們也許可以打 9 折。

lower + risk 降低風險

Recent studies have confirmed that certain types of fish oil can <u>lower the risk of</u> heart disease.
最近的研究證實，某些種類的魚油可以降低心臟病的風險。

lower + rate 降低～率

Some airlines have used this program successfully for decades. It is an effective way to <u>lower the rate of</u> incidents and accidents.
部分航空公司已經成功採用了這套流程數十年，它能有效降低事故發生率。

lower + voice 降低音量

Normally when you visit a museum, you have to <u>lower your voice</u>.
通常在參觀博物館時，必須放低你的音量。

lower + heat 把火調小

<u>Lower the heat</u> to a simmer and let the soup bubble gently, for about 15 minutes.
把火轉小，讓湯慢慢煮滾大約 15 分鐘。

lower + value 降低價值

If the central bank prints more money, each dollar it prints can possibly <u>lower the value of</u> the other dollars out there.
如果央行印更多錢，它印的每一塊錢都可能降低現行貨幣的價值。

lower + standard 降低標準

The company has <u>lowered the standard of</u> living for many of its workers for decades.
幾十年來，這間公司降低了許多員工的生活水準。

Maintain

(maintain — maintained — maintained)

maintain + relationship 保持關係

By <u>maintaining a good relationship with</u> your customers and building trust and loyalty, you are more likely to gain support.
透過與顧客維持良好的關係、建立信任和忠誠度，你更有可能獲得支持。

maintain + contact 保持聯繫

Career center staff <u>maintain contact with</u> young people when they have left school.
就業中心的工作人員在年輕人離開學校後，仍與他們保持聯絡。

maintain + links 保持關係

It's important to develop overseas markets and <u>maintain our links with</u> some of the world's large economies.
開發海外市場並維持我們與世界上一些大型經濟體的關係非常重要。

maintain + standards 維持標準

K-pop idols have a duty to the public to <u>maintain high standards of</u> morality. This is because, in general, pop culture has a huge impact on society.
韓國流行音樂偶像有責任對大眾維持自己的高道德標準。因為一般來說，流行文化對社會有很大的影響。

194

maintain + control 維持控制

The government is trying to <u>maintain control</u> without unduly hampering the market's growth.
政府正嘗試在不過度阻礙市場成長的情況下維持對市場的控制。

maintain + order 維持秩序

The president has the power to use force to <u>maintain public order</u> in times of emergency.
總統有權在緊急情況下使用武力來維持公共秩序。

maintain + position 維持地位

The strategy would help <u>maintain</u> America's <u>position</u> as a leading global force in economic development and innovation for decades to come.
這個策略將有助於在未來數十年，維持美國在全球經濟發展與創新上的領先地位。

maintain + confidentiality 保密

Our employees must be able to <u>maintain confidentiality of</u> customer and company information.
我們的員工必須能夠保住客戶和公司的機密。

Make

▶ MP3-075

(make — made — made)

make + difference 造成影響、改變

Will his management and leadership style <u>make a difference</u>, and if so, how much?
他的管理和領導風格會造成影響嗎？如果會的話，影響有多大？

make + decision 做決定

Given the super typhoon is approaching, many families in mountain areas have to <u>make the tough decision</u> to evacuate.
因為超級颱風即將來襲，許多山區家庭不得不做出撤離的艱難決定。

make + reservation 預約、預訂

If we want to eat out on Chinese New Year's Eve, it's probably wise to <u>make a reservation</u> as soon as possible.
如果我們想要在除夕夜出去吃飯，最好盡快預訂。

make + appointment 預約

I suggest you <u>make an appointment with</u> your dentist and discuss your tooth decay as soon as possible.
我建議你盡快與你的牙醫預約，討論一下你的蛀牙問題。

make + point 強調

I would like to <u>make a point about</u> the importance of
placement tests before I come to the conclusion.
在我做出結論前，我想要強調一下分班考試的重要性。

make + contribution 為～做出貢獻

We should go into markets where we can <u>make a significant
contribution to</u> society, not just sell a lot of products and
make profits.
我們應該投入那些我們可以對社會有重大貢獻的市場，而不只是賣
很多產品賺錢。

make + note 做筆記、記錄

If you don't win the sale, <u>make a note</u> in your calendar to
contact the customer next month.
如果你沒有拿下這筆生意，在你的行事曆上做個紀錄，下個月再聯
繫客戶。

make + call 打電話

He <u>made a call to</u> his assistant during dinner, and said to
him, "I need that file on my desk tomorrow morning at 8
o'clock."
他在吃飯的時候打電話給助理，跟他說：「明天早上 8 點我要那份
文件出現在我桌上。」

make + effort 努力

Such fluctuations in share prices give huge unexpected gains to some, and cause bankruptcy for others. It's high time that the government <u>made an effort to</u> limit the ups and downs.

股價這樣的波動為某些人帶來意想不到的巨大收益,但也導致某些人破產。政府是時候努力限制股市的波動了。

make + progress 進步、取得進展

If we are to <u>make progress in</u> tackling poverty, we have to confront the underlying causes.

如果我們要在解決貧困方面有所進展,我們就必須正視其根本原因。

make + request 提出請求

Employees <u>making a request for</u> flexible work time should consider the business benefits of the arrangement, rather than their personal reasons.

要求彈性工時的員工,應該想想這個安排對公司的好處,而不是他們的個人原因。

make + offer 出價

The house is in a nice neighborhood, but it needs remodeling. Therefore, I <u>made an offer</u> for two-thirds of what they are asking for.

房子所在的地區很棒,但房子本身需要重新裝修。所以我的出價是他們要求價格的三分之二。

make + suggestion 提出建議

You have probably thought of an alternative yourself, so there is no need for me to <u>make a suggestion</u>.
你可能已經有想到替代方案，所以我也沒必要再給建議。

make + bed 整理床鋪

If you grew up the way I did, you would acquire the habit of <u>making your bed</u> before having breakfast.
如果你的成長背景跟我一樣，你就會養成吃早餐前先整理床鋪的習慣。

make + living 謀生

Small business owners are struggling to <u>make a living</u> in such economically hard times, but these CEOs still make billions.
在這個經濟困難的時期，小型企業主們都努力謀生，但這些執行長還是能賺到數十億。

make + profit 獲利、賺錢

Chances are you can <u>make a huge profit on</u> high-risk funds. However, they are more likely to nosedive if the economy turns sour.
你可能可以在高風險基金中獲得很高的報酬，但如果經濟惡化，它們更有可能會暴跌。

make + loss 虧損

A company can <u>make a loss on</u> such a poor business decision.
公司可能會因為這樣一個不好的商業決策而蒙受虧損。

實用短語 / 用法 / 句型

1. make room / space for sth 騰出空間給～

Some hospitals are turning away cancer and heart disease patients to <u>make</u> more <u>room for</u> COVID-19 cases.
有些醫院正拒絕收治癌症及心臟病患者，來騰出更多空間給 COVID-19 的病患。

Meet

▶ MP3-076

(meet — met — met)

meet + needs 滿足需求

Online streaming platforms continue to invest in creating their own shows and movies to <u>meet the needs of</u> their larger users.
線上串流平台持續投資製作自己的節目和電影，來滿足更多用戶的需求。

meet + demands 滿足需求

The company says it is unable to <u>meet the</u> workers' <u>demands for</u> higher wages.
這間公司說，它無法滿足工人希望調高工資的要求。

meet + requirements 滿足要求、符合條件

He was teaching English as a student teacher while taking courses to <u>meet the requirements for</u> his teaching certificate.
他一邊當實習老師教英文，一邊修課來達到教師證書的要求。

meet + conditions 符合條件

If you do not <u>meet</u> all <u>the conditions of</u> your offer, your college can withdraw your offer.
如果你不符合錄取通知上的所有條件，你的學校可以取消你的入學資格。

A
B
C
D
E
F
G
H
I
J
K
L
M
N
O
P
Q
R
S
T
U
V
W

meet + criteria 符合標準

To qualify for a grant, students must <u>meet</u> certain <u>criteria</u> listed in this article.
要獲得獎學金，學生必須符合本文所列的幾項標準。

meet + standards 符合標準

Manufacturers are moving toward more fuel-efficient vehicles and trying to <u>meet the standards of</u> energy efficiency over the course of time.
製造商正在轉向生產更省油的汽車，並試圖最終能達到能源效率標準。

meet + challenges 應對挑戰

We are looking forward to working with schools and the government to <u>meet challenges</u> and take advantage of new opportunities.
我們期待與學校和政府合作，迎接挑戰、好好利用新的機會。

meet + deadline 趕上截止日

Everyone is working extremely hard to <u>meet the deadline for</u> submitting the final project.
為了趕上期末報告的繳交截止日，每個人都非常認真。

meet + goal 達到目標

If a salesperson fails to <u>meet the goals</u>, the company can begin taking steps toward dismissal.
如果銷售人員未達目標，公司可以開始採取解僱措施。

meet + target 達到目標

In this practice, students get a chance to look at where their work didn't go well or where they didn't <u>meet the target</u>.
在這項練習中，學生有機會看到他們哪裡做不好、或是哪裡沒有達到目標。

meet + repayments 還款

We have seen many fresh graduates applying for credit cards, getting them and then going on a spending spree, and being unable to <u>meet the repayments</u>.
我們看過太多剛畢業的學生申請信用卡，拿到之後開始瘋狂花錢，卻無力還款。

meet + cost 支付費用、成本

Many businesses are aiming to claim for loss of earnings as well as help to <u>meet the cost of</u> repairs.
許多企業都打算要求賠償營收損失，同時要求幫助支付修繕費用。

Minimize

(minimize — minimized — minimized)

---

minimize + risk 降低風險

What can be done to <u>minimize the risk</u> that your company may encounter or is encountering now?
如何將公司可能遇到或正在面臨的風險降到最低？

---

minimize + potential 降低可能性

We continue to consult with local political leaders and health officials in an effort to <u>minimize the potential for</u> disease spread.
我們持續與地方首長及衛生官員協商，努力將疾病傳播的可能性降到最低。

---

minimize + possibility 降低可能性

France has taken steps to <u>minimize the possibility</u> that nuclear fuel might be diverted for military purposes.
法國已經採取措施來減少核燃料被轉作軍事目的的可能性。

---

minimize + impact 減輕影響

The financial institution has used a hedging strategy to <u>minimize the impact of</u> currency fluctuations.
這間金融機構採用對沖策略來減輕匯率波動造成的影響。

minimize + effect 減輕影響

Taiwan Power Company notified the authorities before shutting off power to <u>minimize the effect on</u> users.

台灣電力公司在斷電前已經通知相關部門，盡量減少對用戶的影響。

minimize + damage 減少損失

After a typhoon hits, there is a lot we can do by ourselves to <u>minimize the damage</u> rather than waiting for professional help or insurance to kick in.

在颱風來襲後，我們可以自己做很多事情來減少損失，而不是等待專業援助或是保險救助。

minimize + loss 減少損失

The trade war is leaving a tremendous impact on Chinese and Taiwanese tech companies, and our company is preparing for the worst to <u>minimize the loss</u>.

這場貿易戰對中國和臺灣的科技公司造成重大的影響，我們公司正在做最壞的打算以減少損失。

minimize + cost 降低成本

While I understand your desire to <u>minimize the cost of</u> care for your pet, I must also state that people need to trust the advice of their veterinarians.

雖然我理解你想要把照顧寵物的成本降到最低，但我也必須要說，人們要相信獸醫的建議。

minimize + harm 降低傷害

What is most crucial for employers to do to <u>minimize the harm of</u> layoffs?
對雇主來說，要把裁員的傷害降到最低，最關鍵的是什麼？

minimize + number 減少數量（後面接可數名詞）

The supervisors say they want to <u>minimize the number of</u> employees laid off during this financial crisis.
主管們說，他們希望盡量減少在這次金融危機中被解僱的員工人數。

minimize + amount 減少數量（後面接不可數名詞）

Many students work while attending college to <u>minimize the amount of</u> money they will owe when they graduate.
許多學生在大學期間邊工作，盡量減少畢業時欠下的錢。

Mitigate

(mitigate — mitigated — mitigated)

mitigate + effect 減輕影響

Measures need to be taken to <u>mitigate the environmental effects of</u> burning coal to generate electricity.
需要採取措施減輕燃煤發電對環境的影響。

mitigate + impact 減輕影響

TSMC said the company will continue to work with all parties to <u>mitigate the impact of</u> the current automotive chip shortage, a concern shared by automakers around the world.
台積電表示，公司將繼續與各方合作，以減輕目前車用晶片短缺造成的影響，這是全球汽車製作商共同擔心的問題。

mitigate + risk 降低風險

We need more transparency in financial markets. And we have to get financial reform right so that we can <u>mitigate the risk of</u> future meltdowns of the system.
我們需要金融市場有更高的透明度，也必須進行正確的金融改革，這樣我們才能降低體系在未來崩潰的風險。

mitigate + consequence 減輕影響

Facing up to this reality and trying to constructively <u>mitigate the consequences of</u> these choices is something that they have to do.

面對現實、嘗試建設性地減輕這些選擇所造成的影響，是他們必須做的事情。

mitigate + damage 減少損失

The overall aim of the research program is to <u>mitigate the damage</u> caused by earthquakes.

研究計畫的整體目標是減輕地震造成的損害。

mitigate + harm 降低傷害

The government expends trillions of dollars in an effort to <u>mitigate the harm</u> from COVID-19.

政府花了數兆美元來降低 COVID-19 造成的傷害。

Move
(move — moved — moved)

▶ MP3-079

---

move + meeting 更改會議時間

I'm dropping my kids off at school at that time. Let's just
<u>move the meeting from</u> 8:30 <u>to</u> 9:00 o'clock.
那個時間我正在送孩子去學校。我們把會議時間從 8:30 改到 9:00
吧。

實用短語 / 用法 / 句型

1. move mountains 竭盡全力做到非常困難的事
If we get a good team and get all people involved,
we can <u>move mountains to</u> fight COVID.
如果我們有一個好的團隊，讓所有人一同參與，我們就能
對抗新冠狀病毒。

2. move heaven and earth 竭盡全力做到非常困難的事
He vowed that he would <u>move heaven and earth</u> to
finish the project on schedule.
他發誓要竭盡所能地在表定時間完成這項計畫。

3. move the needle 造成顯著的改變
After graduating from Harvard University, he started
his own company, hoping to <u>move the needle</u> in the
pharmaceutical industry.
從哈佛大學畢業後，他創辦了自己的公司，希望為製藥產
業帶來改變。

4. move sb to tears 使某人感動落淚

After several attempts, he finally broke the record set by himself. The success <u>moved him</u> nearly <u>to tears</u>.

他嘗試了好幾次，終於打破自己創下的紀錄。這一成功讓他感動到快哭了。

5. move with the times 與時俱進

As information becomes more readily available in a digital format, publishers are going to have to change their business models if they want to <u>move with the times</u>.

隨著數位形式的資訊越來越容易取得，如果出版商想要與時俱進，他們不得不改變自己的商業模式。

6. not move a muscle 一動也不動

The kids have been glued to the TV all day, <u>not</u> even <u>moving a muscle</u>.

孩子們整天盯著電視，一動也不動。

Navigate

▶ MP3-080

(navigate — navigated — navigated)

navigate + site 瀏覽網站

In terms of searching for specific products, <u>the site</u> is quite easy to <u>navigate</u>. Users can search by price, category, or brand.

在搜尋特定產品方面，這個網站很好用，使用者可以依價格、種類、品牌進行搜尋。

navigate + Internet 瀏覽網路

Many of the Generation Y help their less-fluent parents fill online forms and <u>navigate the Internet</u>.

許多 Y 世代幫助他們不太會操作的父母填寫線上表格以及瀏覽網路。

navigate + system 探索系統

Our healthcare system struggles to give comfort to those suffering, leaving many chronic pain patients to <u>navigate the system</u> and a range of treatment options.

我們的醫療保健系統努力讓那些受病痛折磨的人獲得舒緩，讓許多慢性病患在健保系統和一系列的治療選擇中摸索。

navigate + environment 摸索環境

We'll help you <u>navigate the</u> complex <u>environment of</u> technologies and find the best fitting solutions.

我們將幫助您摸索複雜的技術，並找到最合適的解決方案。

Neglect

(neglect — neglected — neglected)

---

neglect + importance 忽略重要性

Many people tend to <u>neglect the importance of</u> taking care of their mental health. Research shows that women are more prone to mental health disorders than men, but men rarely seek help.

許多人往往忽略了照顧自己心理健康的重要性。研究顯示，女性比男性更容易罹患精神疾病，但男性卻很少尋求幫助。

---

neglect + needs 忽略需求

Because the government has long <u>neglected the needs of</u> gifted students academically, the opportunities for these students have been on the decrease.

由於政府長期以來在學業上忽略了資優生的需求，這些學生的機會一直在減少。

---

neglect + role 忽略～的角色、作用

While there has been much discussion of economic sanctions, we cannot <u>neglect the role of</u> the military in a Plan B.

儘管有很多關於經濟制裁的討論，但我們不能忽略軍方在替代方案中扮演的角色。

neglect + possibility 忽略可能性

Some banks take excessive risks because they <u>neglect the possibility of</u> extreme events or have overly optimistic beliefs.

一些銀行之所以會承擔過多風險，是因為他們忽略了極端事件發生的可能性，或者抱有過度樂觀的想法。

Nourish

(nourish — nourished — nourished)

nourish + skin 滋養皮膚

These products help to <u>nourish</u> and hydrate <u>the skin</u> and provide anti-aging benefits as well.
這些產品有助於滋養和滋潤皮膚，並具有抗老功效。

nourish + soul 滋養心靈

It is important to <u>nourish the soul</u> in a pandemic. Speaking to friends and family on the phone or taking the time to read a book will help you regain power when dealing with anxiety or depression.
在疫情期間，重要的是要滋養心靈。和朋友及家人通個電話或花時間讀本書，會幫助你在處理焦慮或抑鬱時，重新獲得力量。

nourish + body 滋養身體

Eating healthy food—along with getting adequate sleep and exercising—can help <u>nourish the body</u> and maintain a strong immune system.
吃得健康，再加上充足的睡眠和運動，可以幫助滋養身體以及維持強健的免疫系統。

nourish + hair 滋養頭髮

This shampoo penetrates deep into the roots of the hair and the scalp to nourish the hair.

這款洗髮精可以深入髮根和頭皮滋養頭髮。

nourish + children 提供營養給孩子

Speaking of challenges, one of the biggest for parents is weighing our desire to nourish our children against the drudgery of becoming their cooks.

說到挑戰,對父母來說最大的挑戰之一,就是要在餵養孩子以及變成他們廚師的苦差事之間做權衡。

Nurture

▶ MP3-83

(nurture — nurtured — nurtured)

---

nurture + development 培育發展

A supportive environment can <u>nurture the development of</u> teachers who are able to impart up-to-date knowledge to their students.

一個支持性的環境可以培育能夠傳遞學生最新知識的老師。

---

nurture + growth 促進成長

The investment in early education programs will help <u>nurture</u> long-term <u>economic growth</u> and social sustainability.

對幼兒教育計畫的投資,將有助於促進長期的經濟成長和社會的永續發展。

---

nurture + spirit 培育精神

This award recognizes an industry leader who has built successful companies while also helping <u>nurture the spirit of</u> innovation and entrepreneurship.

這個獎項旨在表揚那些建立成功的公司,同時又協助培育創新和創業精神的業界領袖。

nurture + relationship 培養關係

Whatever it is, ensuring that you and your partner have a bit of quality time together will help nurture the relationship.
不論做什麼事情，確保你和伴侶之間有一些美好的時光，有助於培養你們的關係。

nurture + imaginations 培養想像力

In this article, we talk about the benefits of imagination on child development, and explain how parents can further nurture the imaginations of their children.
在這篇文章中，我們討論關於想像力對兒童發展的好處，並解釋父母可以如何進一步培養孩子的想像力。

nurture + talent 培育人才

MIT has a highly structured interview process for hiring professors, and it is designed to extract particular details from applicants, such as their ability to nurture talent.
麻省理工學院在招聘教授時有結構嚴謹的面試過程，目的是從申請人身上得知某些細節，例如他們培育人才的能力。

nurture + potential 培養潛力

The new competence-based education structure seeks to nurture potential by ensuring all learners acquire core skills required for every industry.
這個新的能力本位教育結構，希望透過確保所有學習者都能學會每個產業所需的核心能力，來培養他們的潛力。

Obey

▶ MP3-84

(obey — obeyed — obeyed)

obey + law 遵守法律

Parents have to set a good example in teaching their children to <u>obey the law</u>.
父母必須以身作則，教導子女遵守法律。

obey + rules 遵守規定

Google will require all of its employees to undergo privacy training. The company is also introducing more checks aimed at making sure workers <u>obey the rules</u>.
Google 將要求所有員工都參與隱私相關的訓練。該公司還採取了更多檢查措施，確保員工遵守規定。

obey + orders 服從命令

War criminals tried to justify their actions by saying that they were only <u>obeying orders</u>.
戰犯們說他們只是服從命令，試圖為自己的行為辯護。

obey + command 服從命令

Given that Taliban fighters strictly <u>obeyed the command of</u> their leaders, this high-level talk would make it easier to achieve a ceasefire.
因為塔利班武裝分子嚴格遵從領袖的指揮，這場高層會談將更有機會達成停火。

obey + instructions 遵守指令

The latest variant of online fraud contains a new trick to harvest credit card details. Such emails threaten to close the recipient's account if the recipient does not <u>obey the instructions</u> it gives.

最新的網路詐騙包含一種獲取信用卡資訊的新手法。這類電子郵件會威脅收件人，如果不遵照指示，將關閉其帳戶。

Offer

(offer — offered — offered)

offer + details 提供細節

The central bank said that it would start pursuing new climate-change strategies within the year and will <u>offer details</u> at next month's meeting.

央行表示,今年將採行新的氣候變遷策略,並在下個月的會議上提出細節。

offer + benefit 提供優勢、好處

According to background information in the article, while these medications may <u>offer substantial benefits</u>, there may also be risks.

根據這篇文章的背景資料,雖然這些藥物可能會帶來很大的效益,但也可能存在風險。

offer + services 提供服務

Airbnb now lets hosts <u>offer</u> any kind of experience and <u>services</u> that either last many days or a few hours, not just a bed to sleep in.

Airbnb 現在讓房東可以提供任何形式的體驗和服務,這些體驗和服務可以持續數天或數小時,而不僅僅是一張可以睡覺的床。

offer + product 提供產品

If you need a mortgage loan with a low down payment requirement or your credit is not so pristine, brokers can look for lenders that <u>offer products</u> tailored for your situation.
如果你需要低頭期款的房貸，或者你的信用不是很好，仲介可以依照你的情況尋找提供貸款的機構。

offer + suggestion 提供建議

What <u>practical suggestions</u> can you <u>offer</u> to teachers of children with learning difficulties?
你可以為學習困難兒童的老師提供什麼實質的建議？

offer + advice 提供建議

When <u>offering</u> others <u>advice</u>, we should focus less on the many things we can't fix on our own and more on what we can control.
在給別人建議時，我們應該少注意那些自己無法解決的事情，而是更專注於我們可以控制的事情。

offer + support 提供支持

We <u>offer support to</u> those whose loved ones are suffering from depression. This free program brings us all together to share information and resources across the country.
我們為憂鬱症患者的親人提供支持。這個免費的計畫將大家聚集在一起，分享國內的資訊與資源。

offer + help 提供幫助

After a year and a half of pandemic life, many people are nervous about in-person socialization. Experts are now offering help to those who've forgotten how to hang out.

經過一年半疫情下的生活，許多人對面對面的社交感到緊張。專家們正在為那些忘記如何與人相處的人提供幫助。

offer + assistance 提供幫助

Offering assistance when you notice colleagues are overwhelmed or burdened with a project can help you improve workplace relationships.

當你發現同事對專案感到不知所措或負擔過重時，給予幫忙可以幫助你增進職場關係。

offer + opportunity 提供機會

We treat employees with tremendous respect and offer opportunities for personal growth, competitive salaries, and a generous benefit package.

我們非常尊重員工，並提供個人成長機會、具有競爭力的薪資及優渥的福利。

offer + possibility 提供可能性、機會

Going back to school offers the possibility of joining the labor force when the economy is better. Unemployment rates are also generally lower for people with advanced schooling.

重返校園確實提供了在經濟好轉時找到工作的機會，受過高等教育的人失業率也普遍較低。

offer + chance 提供機會

A farmers market <u>offers the chance to</u> view and sample healthy, homegrown fruits and vegetables.
農夫市集提供了可以逛逛及試吃自產健康蔬果的機會。

實用短語 / 用法 / 句型

1. offer the best rates 提供最好的利率、價格
Post offices, banks and travel operators may be convenient but they don't always <u>offer the best rates of</u> exchange.
郵局、銀行和旅行社換匯可能很方便，但它們提供的匯率不一定最好。

2. offer the best value 提供最高的價值
These equipment suppliers are reputable and <u>offer the best value for money</u>.
這些設備供應商有良好的聲譽，而且提供了絕佳的性價比。

3. offer the best deals 提供最好的交易
The online travel industry is extremely competitive, with players like ezTravel, KKday, and Expedia competing to <u>offer the best deals</u> in airline and hotel bookings.
線上旅遊業競爭非常激烈，易遊網、KKday 和 Expedia 等公司競相提供最優惠的機票和飯店預訂價格。

Omit

▶ MP3-86

(omit — omitted — omitted)

omit + details 遺漏、省略細節

The paper was rejected on the grounds that it had <u>omitted</u> many of the important <u>details</u> related to the experiments.

這篇論文被退稿，理由是它遺漏了許多與實驗有關的重要細節。

omit + word 遺漏、省略文字

Responding to whether the Kuomintang (KMT) would <u>omit the word</u> "Chinese" from its official party name, the chairman of the party said that a name change is not the focus of reform at this stage.

針對國民黨是否會省略正式黨名中的「中國」兩字，黨主席表示，改名不是現階段改革的重點。

omit + fact 忽略事實

If you inadvertently <u>omit an important fact</u>, you and your client will be seen as inept or unresponsive.

如果你不小心忽略了一個重要的事實，你和客戶可能會被認為是能力不足或是反應遲鈍。

omit + factor 忽略因素

The authors <u>omit an important factor</u> here: extensive reading doesn't always result in the improvement of vocabulary knowledge.

作者在這裡忽略了一個重要的因素：廣泛閱讀不見得會提升字彙能力。

Organize

(organize — organized — organized)

organize + information　統整資料

We use computers to store and <u>organize information</u> because it is far better than relying on file clerks and paper documents.
我們用電腦來存放和統整資料，因為這樣做比依賴檔案管理人員和紙本文件要好很多。

organize + document　統整文件

Having an efficient system to file and <u>organize</u> these <u>documents</u> can save a lot of time.
擁有一個高效能的系統來歸檔和統整這些文件，可以大大減少整理文件的時間。

organize + event　組織、籌辦活動

I want to thank all the people who helped to <u>organize</u> this <u>spectacular event</u>. And I'm especially pleased to see many young people who are here.
我要感謝所有幫忙籌辦這次盛會的人。我也很高興看到在座有許多年輕人。

organize + meeting 安排會議

Is there a quick and easy way to <u>organize our next meeting</u> so nobody will get left out?

有沒有快速簡單的方法可以安排我們下一次的會議，這樣就不會有人被遺漏了？

organize + home 整理房子、家

Many of us are working from home as a measure to curb the spread of the deadly virus. Here are five practical tips for <u>organizing your home</u> to enhance productivity and maximize efficiency.

我們有許多人都在家工作，藉此抑制致命病毒的傳播。這裡有五個實用技巧，可以幫助整理你的家、提高生產力、以及大大提升效率。

organize + thoughts 統整想法

You might find that writing an outline will help you <u>organize your thoughts</u>.

你可能會發現寫大綱會幫助你統整想法。

organize + notes 整理筆記

The app includes five templates to help students <u>organize lecture notes</u>, group projects, events, courses and even their job searches.

這個應用程式有五種模板，幫助學生整理課堂筆記、分組報告、活動、課程，甚至他們的求職資料。

organize + finances 整理財務

She gets paid to help clients streamline emails, <u>organize finances</u>, manage documents and photos and back them all up.

她的工作是幫助客戶簡化電子郵件、整理財務狀況、管理文件及照片，並將這些資料做備份。

Outline

(outline — outlined — outlined)

outline + trends 概述趨勢

The <u>trends outlined</u> above have no doubt made that prospect more appealing , but a deal will not be easy to pull off.
上述趨勢無疑使這個前景變得更有吸引力，但要達成協議並不容易。

outline + steps 列出步驟、措施

The central bank said it is watching house prices carefully and the finance minister in December <u>outlined steps</u> he could take to cool things down, if needed.
央行表示正在密切關注房價，財政部長也在 12 月列出了必要時可以讓房市降溫的作法。

outline + principles 概述原則

This branding experience has led to the creation of <u>the basic principles outlined</u> in this report.
這次的品牌推廣經驗帶出了這份報告中列舉的基本原則。

outline + features 概述特點

The following article <u>outlined the main features of</u> what we, as a result of our theoretical and empirical studies, have come to regard as desirable learning materials.
根據我們的理論和實證研究結果，下面這篇文章概述了我們認為理想的學習教材該有的主要特點。

outline + points 列出要點

In advance of his visit, Simon Sinek has <u>outlined the main points about</u> *The Infinite Game* to help readers frame their questions.

在訪問之前，Simon Sinek 列出了關於《無限賽局》（The Infinite Game）一書的要點，以幫助讀者提出問題。

outline + plan 概述計畫

The tax <u>plan</u> I <u>outlined</u> has features that are attractive to both parties, and thus provides a road map for a future consensus.

我列出的稅收計畫具有對兩黨都有吸引力的特點，因此也為雙方未來要達成的共識提供了方向。

outline + responsibilities 列出責任

The duties and <u>responsibilities outlined</u> in this position may be added to or changed when deemed appropriate and necessary.

在認為適當且必要時，可以增加或更改該職位所列出的義務和責任。

outline + need 概述需求

In this document, the public works director has <u>outlined the need for</u> more money for streets.

在這份文件中，公共工程主任簡述了修建街道需要更多的資金。

outline + progress 概述進展

Obama <u>outlined his progress</u> during the first term and asked for supporters' help in the upcoming campaign.
Obama 概述了他在第一個任期內的進展，並尋求支持者在即將到來的競選活動中的幫忙。

Overcome

▶ MP3-89

(overcome — overcame — overcome)

overcome + fear 克服恐懼

She was struggling to <u>overcome fear</u> and self-doubt. But she never shied away from standing up for what she believed in.
她努力克服恐懼和自我懷疑。但她從來不怕捍衛自己的信仰。

overcome + shyness 克服害羞

Most universities will let you stay in halls of residence for the first year. The key to survival is to be yourself and try to <u>overcome</u> any <u>shyness</u> you may have.
多數大學第一年會讓你住宿舍。生存下來的關鍵是要做自己，並試著克服你的害羞。

overcome + obstacle 克服阻礙

If these <u>obstacles</u> can <u>be overcome</u>, then the biggest winner will be the patient.
如果能夠克服這些阻礙，病患將會是最大贏家。

overcome + problem 克服問題

We need a competent government to <u>overcome the thorny problems</u> we face. Hopefully this prime minister will convince the donors to send more aid and help set infrastructure.
我們需要一個有能力的政府來克服我們面臨的難題。希望這位總理能夠說服捐助國提供更多援助以及幫助建立基礎設施。

overcome + difficulty 克服困難

I believe we have the power to <u>overcome the difficulties of</u> economic and budget pressures.
我相信我們有能力克服經濟和預算壓力的難關。

overcome + resistance 克服反對

They are trying to <u>overcome resistance</u> from members who question the wisdom of walking off the job during a recession.
他們正在努力克服一些成員的反對，這些成員質疑在經濟衰退期間辭職是否明智。

overcome + poverty 克服貧窮

Nations must act fast to prevent the global rise in food prices from hurting efforts to help developing countries <u>overcome poverty</u> and hunger.
各國必須迅速採取行動，防止因為全球糧食價格上漲，損害為了幫助發展中國家克服貧窮和飢荒所付出的努力。

overcome + lack 克服不足

Policymakers want to free up credit but have yet to <u>overcome the lack of</u> confidence that has virtually halted lending among banks.

政策制定者希望放寬信用貸款，但尚未克服導致銀行幾乎停止放貸的信心不足問題。

overcome + weakness 克服弱點、缺點

The survey suggests that the economy is gaining momentum and has not yet <u>overcome weaknesses in</u> banking and employment.

調查顯示，這個經濟體正蓄勢待發，但尚未克服銀行業和就業方面的不足。

overcome + enemy 戰勝敵人

Online games, such as World of Warcraft, require players to collaborate with one another, forging alliances and developing common strategies to <u>overcome the enemy</u>.

像《魔獸世界》（World of Warcraft）這樣的線上遊戲，要求玩家相互合作、結盟、訂定共同的策略來戰勝敵人。

Oversee

▶ MP3-90

(oversee — oversaw — overseen)

oversee + implementation 監督執行狀況

A new committee will <u>oversee the implementation of</u> the plan, though it's not yet known who will lead it, how many are on it, or how long it will run for.
新的委員會將監督這個計畫的執行狀況,但目前還不清楚會由誰帶領這個計畫、有多少人參與、以及計畫會持續多久。

oversee + development 監督發展、進展

Based mostly at the hotels, these specialists are change agents who help <u>oversee the development of</u> projects.
這些大多在飯店裡工作的專家是促進改革的顧問,協助監督專案的進展。

oversee + work 監督工作、作業

Having so many people coming from other departments to <u>oversee the work</u> blurred the lines of specific responsibilities.
有這麼多其他部門的人來監督工作,模糊了具體職責的界線。

oversee + project 監督專案

The city plans to select a master developer to <u>oversee the project</u> as early as next month.
該城市計劃最快在下個月挑選一位主要開發商來監督這個專案。

oversee + process　監督流程

A project manager has been appointed to <u>oversee the process</u>, and over the next two weeks working groups for each part will be created.

一位專案經理被任命來監督這個流程,並在接下來的兩週內為每個階段成立工作小組。

oversee + operation　監督操作

Customers can pay for items using something like a credit card or a mobile payment at a computer kiosk. Security cameras will <u>oversee the operation</u> to keep everyone honest.

顧客結帳時可以在自助結帳機刷信用卡或使用行動支付。監視器會監控結帳過程,確保大家都誠實。

oversee + activities　監督活動

The committee is responsible for <u>overseeing activities</u> ranging from investing pension funds to building affordable housing.

這個委員會負責監督從退撫基金投資到負擔得起的住宅建設等各項活動。

oversee + management　監督管理

The company will <u>oversee the management of</u> the project, including its 48 unsold residential units and one commercial unit.

這間公司將監督該專案的管理,此專案包含 48 個未售出的一般住宅和 1 個商業住宅。

Overthrow

▶ MP3-91

(overthrow — overthrew — overthrown)

overthrow + government 推翻政府

The movement seeks to <u>overthrow the government</u> to improve the lives of the poor.
這場活動的目的是推翻政府，以改善窮人的生活。

overthrow + regime 推翻政權

Will the Iranian people rise up and <u>overthrow the regime</u> because of the sanctions that make their daily lives difficult?
伊朗人民會因為制裁使他們的日常生活變得困難，而起來推翻政權嗎？

overthrow + system 推翻體制、制度

One wing sought reform of the capitalist system, while the other sought to <u>overthrow the system</u> entirely.
一派主張改革資本主義制度，然而另一派主張徹底推翻資本主義制度。

Perform
▶ MP3-92

(perform — performed — performed)

perform + work 執行工作

Discrimination against female employees still occurs in workplaces—women who <u>perform the</u> same <u>work</u> as men do not receive equal pay and equal benefits.
職場上仍然有對女性員工的歧視，她們與男性做相同的工作，卻得不到同等的薪資和福利。

perform + task 執行任務

Scientists report that the degree of change reflects how well the machine has learned from experience to <u>perform tasks</u>.
科學家們報告説，改變的程度反映出機器從經驗中學到多少執行任務的能力。

perform + job 執行工作

Anyone who is interested in this position must have the necessary skills, including sound reasoning ability when making decisions, to <u>perform the job</u> well.
任何對這個職位有興趣的人，都必須具備應有的技能，包括做決策時良好的推理能力，來做好這份工作。

perform + duty 履行職責、義務

If you can <u>perform your duty</u> and meet the required standard, it doesn't matter what your gender is.
如果你能完成職責並達到要求的標準，那麼你的性別就不重要。

perform + function 執行功能

This global semiconductor foundry company is a leader in providing various chips designed to <u>perform</u> very specific <u>functions</u>.
這家全球半導體代工公司在提供各種用於執行特定功能的晶片方面處於領先地位。

perform + role 扮演～的角色、作用

The external stressors in our lives often <u>perform a vital role in</u> our physical, mental and emotional growth.
生活中的外部壓力往往對我們的身體、心理和情感成長扮演著重要的角色。

perform + service 執行服務

We <u>perform services</u> that help you design insurance and retirement plans.
我們提供幫助你規劃保險和退休計畫的服務。

perform + action 執行操作

If you are wondering how to link your passport with COVID-19 vaccination certificate, here are the steps you can follow to <u>perform the action</u>.
如果你想知道如何將護照與 COVID-19 疫苗接種證明連結在一起，你可以按照以下步驟操作。

perform + analysis 進行分析

These researchers reviewed the data and <u>performed</u> their own <u>statistical analysis</u>.
這些研究人員看了數據，並進行自己的統計分析。

perform + experiment 進行實驗

If there is any truth to these theories, then why not <u>perform the experiment</u> that will provide the data to back them up and then publish the results?
如果這些理論是真的，那為什麼不進行實驗，提供數據來支持理論，接著發表結果呢？

perform + operation 進行操作；執行手術

There are many ways to <u>perform an operation</u>, but different approaches may have different outcomes.
執行手術的方法有很多種，但不同的方法可能會有不同的結果。

perform + ceremony 主持典禮

Jenny and I have decided to get married, and we would be honored if you would <u>perform the ceremony</u>.

Jenny 和我決定要結婚了，如果你可以主持婚禮，我們會覺得很榮幸。

perform + miracle 創造奇蹟

As we all know, <u>miracles can be performed</u> but the cost of cancer treatment is becoming prohibitive.

我們都知道，奇蹟是有可能創造出來的，但治療癌症的費用卻越來越高。

Place
(place — placed — placed)

place + advertisement 投放廣告、刊登廣告

If you would like to <u>place an advertisement</u> in this group, please do so but keep posts short.
如果你想在社團裡刊登廣告，歡迎你這麼做，但貼文請保持簡短。

place + bet 打賭、押注

Rumor has it that plenty of speculators tapped their home equity to <u>place a bet on</u> shipping stocks as the stock prices are rising.
據說隨著股價上漲，許多投機客利用房子資產押注航運股。

place + order 下訂單

If you are outside of our delivery radius you can still <u>place an order</u> via UberEats to collect directly from the restaurant.
如果您不在我們的外送範圍內，您仍然可以透過 UberEats 下訂單，直接到餐廳自行取餐。

place + bid 出價

Some of the biggest banking institutions were expected to <u>place a bid</u>, but it was unclear which ones will.
一些最大的銀行機構預計會出價收購，但目前仍不清楚是哪幾家。

place + burden 造成負擔

The flood of questions from consumers about the impact of policy changes is already starting to <u>place a huge burden on</u> operations.
消費者對於政策改變造成的影響所提出的大量問題，已經開始為公司營運帶來巨大負擔。

place + blame 指責、咎責

The restaurant owner <u>placed the blame on</u> the government policy that encouraged people to stay home during the pandemic.
餐廳老闆將責任歸咎於政府鼓勵民眾疫情期間待在家的政策。

place + emphasis 強調、重視

Learning and teaching for the sheer joy of it is not acceptable due to societal expectations that <u>place emphasis on</u> competition over learning.
單純為了快樂而學習和教學是不被接受的，因為社會期望強調競爭而不是學習。

place + priority 優先考量

To achieve these goals we <u>place a high priority on</u> our relationships with employees, customers and suppliers.
為了實現這些目標，我們非常重視與員工、客戶和供應商的關係。

place + value 重視

Asians tend to <u>place a high value on</u> education, inadvertently creating a competitive, rather than supportive, atmosphere in the classroom.

亞洲人往往極為重視教育，無意間便營造出一種競爭而非相互支持的班級氣氛。

Pose

▶ MP3-94

(pose — posed — posed)

pose + threat 造成威脅

Two storm systems to the southeast of Taiwan have a chance to become tropical storms in the coming days, but it is unclear at this point whether they would <u>pose a threat to</u> Taiwan.

臺灣東南方的兩個低壓系統有機會在未來幾天成為熱帶低壓，但目前還不清楚它們是否會對臺灣造成威脅。

pose + risk 帶來風險

The recent rise in housing prices <u>pose a major risk to</u> the domestic economy.

近期房價上漲對國內經濟帶來重大風險。

pose + danger 帶來、造成危險

Mild cases of the flu can still <u>pose a danger to</u> others.

流感的輕症病例仍會對他人造成危險。

pose + problem 帶來問題

He adds that some schools offer scholarships just for senior students. That is, there are some restrictions that may <u>pose a problem for</u> some junior athletes.

他補充說，有些學校只提供獎學金給高年級學生，也就是說，有一些限制可能會對某些低年級的運動員造成問題。

pose + challenge 帶來挑戰

We recognize that these developments <u>pose a challenge for</u> the countries and regions concerned and also for the international community.

我們認知到，這些情勢發展對於相關國家和區域以及國際社會帶來挑戰。

pose + question 提出問題

This is the second section of today's workshop where we can <u>pose questions to</u> industry and academic leaders.

這是今天研討會的第二部分，我們可以向業界和學界領袖提問。

Possess

▶ MP3-95

(possess — possessed — possessed)

possess + ability 具備能力

The candidate must <u>possess the ability to</u> multitask in a fast paced environment. Bookkeeping and advanced computer skills including advanced use of Microsoft Office Suite are required.

應徵者必須具備在節奏快的環境中多工處理事情的能力。記帳和進階的電腦處理能力，包含 Microsoft Office 軟體的熟練應用，都是必備的。

possess + skills 具備技能

At the same time, they also <u>possess strong language skills</u> and a solid technical background.

同時他們也具備了很強的語言能力，且擁有扎實的技術背景。

possess + power 具有能力、權力

They <u>possess the power to</u> veto many development projects that could provide us all with jobs.

他們有權否決許多可以為我們所有人帶來工作的開發計畫。

possess + knowledge 具備知識

Many employees lack the knowledge to save money, or else possess the knowledge but lack the motivation to participate in retirement savings plans.
許多員工缺乏儲蓄的概念，或者是具備這樣的知識但卻缺乏加入退休儲蓄計畫的動力。

possess + eligibility 具備資格

Candidates responding to this post must currently possess the eligibility to work in the United States.
回覆這篇職缺的應徵者，目前必須具備在美國工作的資格。

possess + qualifications 具備資格、條件

Individuals who possess the following qualifications are encouraged to submit a resume and a cover letter outlining their relevant experience.
我們鼓勵具備以下資格的人繳交履歷和求職信，簡述自己的相關經驗。

possess + potential 具有潛力

Stem cells are used in this research because they possess the potential to transform into specific types of cells needed by particular organs.
幹細胞被應用於這項研究中，因為它們具有轉化成特定器官所需的特定類型細胞的潛力。

Preserve

▶ MP3-96

(preserve — preserved — preserved)

preserve + environment 保護環境

The city would seek to balance the public's reaction to the proposed expressway project and the need to <u>preserve the environment</u>.

該市將在民眾對高速公路計畫的反應和環境保護的必要性之間尋求平衡。

preserve + integrity 保存完整性

The economist stressed that the move wasn't a bailout but an effort to <u>preserve the integrity of</u> the overall financial system.

這位經濟學家強調，此舉不是紓困，而是努力維護整個金融體系的完整性。

preserve + value 保存價值

Given inflation rates, cash will lose nearly half of its value over 20 years. Long-term investors need more robust strategies to <u>preserve the value of</u> savings.

考量到通貨膨脹率，現金將在 20 年後貶值近一半。長期投資者需要更穩健的策略來維持存款的價值。

preserve + character 保存特色

We've been trying hard to <u>preserve the character of</u> the town, and that's one of the ways we're pushing back on the developer.
我們一直在努力保存這個城鎮的特色，這也是我們抵制開發商的方式之一。

preserve + peace 維護和平

Finding a candidate who can <u>preserve the peace of</u> the community and do a convincing job will be a tall order.
要找到一個能夠維護社區和平並做得令人信服的候選人，是件很難的事。

preserve + resources 保護資源

Let's develop environmental strategies that not only <u>preserve</u> our <u>natural resources</u> but also enhance our quality of life and economic standing.
我們來制定不只能保護自然資源、也能提高生活品質和經濟地位的環境策略吧。

實用短語 / 用法 / 句型

1. preserve the status quo 維持現狀
Farmers cosseted by high barriers to imports are keen to <u>preserve the status quo</u>.
受到關稅壁壘過度保護的農民，都非常希望維持現狀。

Produce

(produce — produced — produced)

produce + results 產生結果

Even the most rigorously adhered-to diet will not <u>produce the same results</u> from person to person. Some of us are simply genetically predisposed to burn calories more efficiently than others.

即使是嚴格遵守飲食計畫，結果也會因人而異。有些人天生就比其他人更容易燃燒卡路里。

produce + effect 產生效果

While most antibodies eventually led to poor survival rates in the lab mice, one particular antibody managed to <u>produce the intended effect</u>.

雖然多數抗體最終造成實驗鼠的存活率偏低，但有一種抗體成功產生了預期的效果。

produce + report 提出、做報告

A committee studying the feasibility of the long-delayed Taipei Dome is expected to <u>produce a report</u> this year.

委員會正在研究延宕已久的臺北大巨蛋的可行性，預期今年會提出一份報告。

produce + products　生產產品

Over the last four decades, Apple has <u>produced</u> many innovative <u>products</u> in the technology industry.
過去 40 年裡，蘋果公司生產了許多在科技業中創新的產品。

produce + goods　生產產品

Usually Toyota and other large manufacturers <u>produce goods</u> based on incoming orders and forecasts for those sales. Now due to the global chip shortage, it's producing based on what parts are available.
通常豐田和其他汽車製造大廠會根據新訂單和預期銷量來生產產品。目前由於全球晶片短缺，豐田只能用現有零件進行生產。

produce + evidence　提出證據

The retired firefighters have been required to <u>produce evidence</u> to prove that a specific event caused their post-traumatic stress disorder (PTSD).
這些退役消防員被要求提出證據，以證明特定事件造成他們罹患創傷後壓力症候群（PTSD）。

produce + film　製作電影

The crew have a week to <u>produce the film</u>, but have to shoot all the scenes in 12 hours today.
團隊有一個禮拜的時間來製作這部電影，但今天必須在 12 小時內拍完所有場景。

Prohibit

▶ MP3-98

(prohibit — prohibited — prohibited)

prohibit + use 禁止使用

While the ban prohibits campfires, it does not <u>prohibit the use of</u> barbecue grills.
雖然明文禁止營火，但並沒有禁止使用烤肉架。

prohibit + sale 禁止販售

We are updating our regulated goods policy to <u>prohibit the sale of</u> alcohol and tobacco products between private individuals on Facebook and Instagram.
我們正在更新商品規範政策，以禁止個人在 Facebook 和 Instagram 上販售菸酒產品。

prohibit + importation 禁止進口

The US offers support for the Australian bill that would <u>prohibit the importation of</u> goods from Xinjiang province and other areas using forced labor.
美國表示支持澳洲法案，該法案將禁止從新疆省及其他有強迫勞動行為的地區進口產品。

prohibit + export 禁止出口

The government <u>prohibited the export of</u> masks just four days after identifying the first confirmed case and started to install additional mask production lines.
政府在發現首例確診案例後短短 4 天，就禁止口罩出口，並開始增設口罩產線。

prohibit + release 禁止發布

Privacy laws <u>prohibit the release</u> of any names without permission from the winner of the lottery prize.
隱私法禁止在未經彩券中獎人允許的情況下公布任何姓名。

Pull

▶ MP3-99

(pull — pulled — pulled)

---

pull + prank 惡作劇

After being treated at the hospital, the students told officers they were simply trying to <u>pull a prank</u> they'd seen on YouTube.

在醫院接受治療後，學生們告訴警察，他們是嘗試模仿在 YouTube 上看到的惡作劇。

實用短語 / 用法 / 句型

1. pull the trigger 扣板機（開槍）；做出決定、採取行動（可能造成後續影響）

Our vaccination program has really improved and so many people have received their booster. Once they are, it can really help them <u>pull the trigger on</u> their decision to travel.

我們的疫苗接種計畫實際上有所改善，現在很多人都已經完成第二劑接種。一旦他們完成接種，確實可以幫助他們決定是否要去旅行。

2. pull strings 幕後牽線、動用關係、走後門

If you're from a low-income household, you're less likely to have the kind of family connections who can <u>pull strings to</u> get you an interview at Google, Facebook, a major bank or a fashion magazine.

如果你來自低收入家庭，靠親戚關係幫你牽線，替你拿到 Google、Facebook、大型銀行、或是時尚雜誌的面試機會是比較低的。

3. pull the plug 停止做～

If the viewing figures drop much more, our YouTube channel will probably <u>pull the plug on</u> the whole series.
如果觀看次數持續下滑，我們的 YouTube 頻道可能不會再做這個系列的影片。

4. pull the wool over one's eyes 矇騙某人

Don't hold anything back or try to <u>pull the wool over</u> customers' <u>eyes</u> when doing business today.
當今在做生意的時候，不要有所隱瞞、也不要試圖欺騙消費者。

5. pull the rug out 突然停止對某人的幫助、支持

Innovation and competitive advantages, among other factors, regularly crown new superstars, such as Tesla and Netflix, and <u>pull the rug out from under</u> other companies.
創新和競爭優勢，在其他的因素當中，經常為特斯拉、Netflix 這類的新起之秀加冕，搶走其他公司所受到的注意。

6. pull a stunt 做愚蠢、危險的事

I will be pissed off if someone <u>pulls a stunt</u> like that. Why would anyone trust someone who thinks trickery is acceptable?
如果有人做這種蠢事，我會很不爽。為什麼會有人相信一個認為欺騙行為是可以接受的人？

7. pull an all-nighter 開夜車（熬夜讀書、工作）

I haven't been able to finish my homework and actually there's a lot left. I think I might have to <u>pull an all-nighter</u>.
我還沒做完作業，事實上還剩很多。我想我可能要熬夜了。

Pursue

(pursue — pursued — pursued)

A
B
C
D
E
F
G
H
I
J
K
L
M
N
O
P
Q
R
S
T
U
V
W

pursue + matter 追究事情

The lawyer said the police would not <u>pursue the matter</u> any
further because no one has come forward and because of a
lack of physical evidence.
律師表示，由於沒有人站出來、也缺乏物證，警方將不會進一步追
查此事。

pursue + career 追求事業

What advice would you give to schoolchildren wishing to
<u>pursue a career in</u> sports?
你會給希望以體育運動做為職涯發展的學生什麼建議？

pursue + degree 攻讀學位

My passion for language teaching and learning prompted
me to <u>pursue a degree in</u> second language acquisition.
我對語言教學與學習的熱情促使我攻讀第二語言習得的學位。

pursue + goal 追求目標

The finding provides insight into the way people <u>pursue their
goals</u> and how motivation drives goal-oriented behavior.
這一發現讓我們深入了解人們追求目標的方式、以及動機如何驅使
目標導向的行為。

pursue + opportunity 尋求機會

Regardless of the continuing labor shortage, especially specialized and qualified workforce, we're still seeing many young people leaving the country to <u>pursue opportunities</u> abroad.

即使國內的勞動力短缺，特別是專業和合格人力不足，我們還是看到許多年輕人出國尋找機會。

pursue + interest 追求興趣

While working from home during the pandemic, I have a chance to <u>pursue</u> some <u>interests</u> I haven't really had a chance to do.

疫情期間在家工作的我，有機會去嘗試一些以前沒有機會追求的興趣。

pursue + idea 實行想法

If residents and business owners show support for the concept, community officials will <u>pursue the idea of</u> urban renewal.

如果居民和店家支持這個想法，社區管理委員就會著手都市更新。

pursue + policy 採取政策

We know the media magnate's intent was to influence decision-makers to <u>pursue policies</u> that favored his business.

我們知道這位媒體大亨的目的是影響決策者，使他們採取對自家企業有利的政策。

pursue + development 追求發展

Our new partnership with MediaTek, which was announced Wednesday, will <u>pursue the development of</u> innovative technologies in electronics and energy efficiency.

我們於週三宣布與聯發科建立新的合作夥伴關係，將致力於開發電子和能源效率方面的創新技術。

Push

(push — pushed — pushed)

push + boundaries 挑戰極限、界線

If you are visiting London and you like things that are creative and <u>push boundaries</u>, this is the place to come. I don't know if the food is as up to scratch as the others, but for atmosphere and value for money, this is hard to beat.
如果你正在倫敦旅遊，而且喜歡有創意、挑戰極限的東西，那你一定要來這個地方。我不知道這裡的食物是否跟其他餐廳一樣好，但就氣氛和性價比而言，這裡完勝其他地方。

push + limits 挑戰極限

We surround ourselves with a team of forward-thinking professionals who aren't afraid to <u>push the limits</u>.
我們的團隊都是有遠見、不怕挑戰極限的專業人士。

實用短語 / 用法 / 句型

1. push one's buttons 惹毛某人

No one will be able to <u>push your buttons</u> like your children, but it's all a part of the challenges of parenthood.
沒人有辦法像你的小孩一樣惹毛你，但這都是為人父母會遇到的一部分挑戰。

2. push the envelope 挑戰極限

Companies like Nike and Apple take greater risks and push the envelope in pursuit of innovation with their entrepreneurial spirit.

像是 Nike 和蘋果這樣的公司冒著更大的風險，憑著創業家精神挑戰極限、追求創新。

3. push sth out of one's mind / to the back of one's mind 把～忘掉、把～拋諸腦後

The dish was good enough to push the diet to the back of my mind.

這道菜好吃到讓我把減肥暫時擺一邊。

4. push sb to the wall 逼得某人沒有退路

If the government continues pushing its citizens to the wall, it shouldn't be surprised when they rise up.

如果政府繼續把民眾逼得退無可退，那麼當他們群起反抗時也不用驚訝。

5. push one's luck 指望好運會持續、冒更多的險

Using leverage to trade stocks will result in unrecoverable losses, and you probably don't want to push your luck any further.

使用槓桿進行股票交易可能會造成難以挽回的虧損，你不應該再冒更多的險。

6. to be pushed for money 經濟拮据、手頭緊

I am kind of pushed for money right now, so can we go out for dinner next weekend instead?

我現在手頭有點緊，我們能不能改成下週末再出去吃晚餐？

Put

▶ MP3-102

(put — put — put)

put + energy 投入精力

There are social problems that seem intractable, but when we <u>put energy into</u> pushing back, we are able to change things.
有些社會問題看似難以解決，但當我們投入精力試圖解決時，我們就能做出改變。

put + effort 付出努力

We've <u>put</u> a lot of <u>effort into</u> this program, and we're looking forward to the outcome of our efforts.
我們在這個計畫上付出了很多努力，期待看到我們努力的成果。

put + emphasis 強調、重視

Under the threat of the coronavirus, people have begun to <u>put more emphasis on</u> health and have better understood the significance of disease prevention.
在這次新冠肺炎的威脅下，大家更重視健康，體認到疾病預防的重要性。

put + price 估價

You can't <u>put a price on</u> what a mother does for her children.
你無法用金錢來衡量母親為孩子所做的一切。

put + value 估價、估值

The further away you get from the idea of predictable business, the harder it gets to put a value on a company.
生意越是無法預測,就越難計算一家公司的估值。

put + money 投入金錢

Some investors hesitate to put money into China because they are worried about government intervention in the market.
有些投資人對投資中國持保留態度,因為他們擔心政府對市場的干預。

put + pressure 施加壓力

Celebrities' popularity often comes at a price. We put a lot of pressure on these people and expect them to never make mistakes.
名人會受歡迎往往是有代價的。我們給這些人很大的壓力,期待他們永遠不會犯錯。

put + strain 施加壓力

It is said that starting a company with a friend, sibling, or spouse can easily put a strain on personal relationships.
據說和朋友、兄弟姊妹、配偶一起創業,容易造成關係緊張。

put + blame 指責、咎責

The public seems to be <u>putting the blame for</u> the data breach <u>on</u> the company's lax security measures.
民眾似乎把資料外洩的責任歸咎於公司鬆懈的安全措施。

put + question 提出問題

We've got a few minutes for questions. I don't know if anyone would like to <u>put a question to</u> our speaker today.
我們還有幾分鐘的時間可以提問，不知道有沒有人有問題想請教我們今天的講者。

實用短語 / 用法 / 句型

1. put a damper on sth 打亂、擾亂～

There is going to be a downpour of rain, and we worry that this will <u>put a damper on</u> our event this week.
要下大雨了，我們擔心這會打亂我們這週的活動。

2. put sb / sth at risk 使～身陷危險

As hackers get smarter and computers get more powerful, national security <u>is</u> now <u>put at risk</u>.
隨著駭客越來越聰明、電腦越來越強大，現在國家安全處於危險之中。

3. put sth into practice 把～付諸實踐

Reading and enjoying *Atomic Habits* is one thing, putting all of the principles into practice is quite another.

閱讀和享受《原子習慣》（Atoimc Habits）是一回事，把書裡的所有法則付諸實踐又是另一回事。

4. put sth into effect 使～生效

Community members will be voting on the regulation in a few weeks. If passed, it will be put into effect soon after.

社區成員將在幾週內對這項規定進行投票，如果通過，很快就會生效。

5. put an end / a stop to sth 停止、結束～

The Biden administration would do well to ensure that a comprehensive trade agreement is reached with China so as to put an end to the trade war once and for all.

拜登政府將努力確保與中國達成全面的貿易協定，進而徹底結束貿易戰。

Quash

▶ MP3-103

(quash — quashed — quashed)

quash + revolt 鎮壓叛亂

The government of Hong Kong imposed even harsher measures to try to <u>quash the revolt</u>.
香港政府實施更嚴格的措施來試圖鎮壓叛亂。

quash + speculation 停止、駁斥猜測

The President <u>quashed the speculation</u> that the Bank's monetary policy committee had decided to wrap up quantitative easing.
央行總裁駁斥了有關外界對於貨幣政策委員會決定結束量化寬鬆的猜測。

quash + decision 撤銷決定

The decision maker may need to analyze the basis on which the previous <u>decision was quashed</u> and take into account the parts of the decision unaffected by the quashing.
決策者可能需要分析先前決定被撤銷的依據，並將未受撤銷決定影響的部分列入考量。

quash + conviction 撤銷判決

His first <u>conviction was quashed</u> on appeal for lack of evidence.
由於證據不足，他的一審判決在上訴後被撤銷。

Quell

▶ MP3-104

(quell — quelled — quelled)

quell + fears 消除擔憂、恐懼

Health officials are trying to <u>quell public fears about</u> rising COVID-19 infections in the area after a spike in confirmed cases over the weekend.
上週末的確診病例數激增，衛生官員正努力平息民眾對於該地區 COVID-19 感染人數上升的擔憂。

quell + unrest 鎮壓暴動、平息動盪

Anger over high food prices has sparked protests in several countries. To <u>quell unrest</u>, countries including Indonesia are digging deep to boost food subsidies.
對於高物價的怒火，已經在幾個國家引起抗議。為了平息動盪，包括印尼在內的一些國家正大力提高食物補貼。

quell + uprising 鎮壓暴動

China vowed to defend its sovereignty in Tibet as Chinese troops set up checkpoints and mobilized to <u>quell the uprising</u>.
中國軍隊在西藏設立檢查站，並動員軍隊鎮壓暴動，誓言捍衛其在西藏的主權。

quell + violence 鎮壓暴力事件

As stores were looted and windows were smashed during protests, the government responded by ordering the army to help police <u>quell the violence</u>.

由於在抗議過程中商店遭搶劫、窗戶被砸碎，政府做出回應，命令軍隊協助警察鎮壓暴力事件。

quell + disturbance 鎮壓暴動

Authorities called in dozens of armored personnel carriers and other vehicles to help <u>quell the disturbance</u>, which lasted for hours.

當局召集了數十輛裝甲運兵車和其他車輛，來協助鎮壓這場持續了數小時的暴動。

Quench

▶ MP3-105

(quench — quenched — quenched)

quench + fire 澆熄、撲滅火焰

Firefighters <u>quenched</u> the remains of <u>the fire</u> and property damage is estimated at US$50,000.
消防隊員將殘餘火勢撲滅，財產損失估計為 5 萬美元。

quench + thirst 解渴；滿足渴望

It's such a scorcher today. I drank two bottles of water to <u>quench my thirst</u>.
今天太熱了，我喝了兩瓶水來解渴。

quench + desire 滿足渴望

I would like to express my gratitude to those who have guided me on my never ending search to <u>quench my desire for</u> knowledge and personal growth within this incredible sport.
我想感謝那些指引我在這項這麼棒的運動中不斷探索、滿足我對知識和自我成長渴望的人。

Raise

▶ MP3-106

(raise — raised — raised)

raise + awareness 提高意識

The student group aims to <u>raise awareness of</u> same-sex
marriage by initiating discussion on the issue in the open.
這個學生團體旨在透過公開討論同性婚姻，來提高民眾對這個議題
的認識。

raise + possibility 提高可能性

Recent military moves in the South China Sea and the
Taiwan Strait <u>raise the possibility of</u> actual clashes between
the two countries, intended or not.
最近在南海和臺灣海峽的軍事行動，都有意無意地增加了兩國之間
發生實際衝突的可能性。

raise + price 漲價

The sluggish economy is limiting the ability of many
companies to <u>raise prices</u>.
經濟不景氣限制了許多公司調漲價格的能力。

raise + taxes 增稅

Faced with a huge budget deficit, officials want to <u>raise taxes on</u> the wealthy, but the elected representative thinks there is another way to raise revenues.
面對巨額預算赤字，官員想對富人增稅，但這位民選代表認為有其他增加收入的方法。

raise + profile 提升形象、知名度

With fresh demand growing for individual sports such as running and workouts amid the pandemic, companies should make use of social media to <u>raise the profile of</u> their products.
隨著疫情期間對跑步和健身等個人運動的需求增加，公司應該利用社群媒體來提高產品知名度。

raise + standards 提高標準

We are determined to <u>raise living standards</u> and give our children the best education.
我們努力提高生活水平，並提供我們孩子最好的教育。

raise + game 提升表現

That strongly held belief enabled him to <u>raise his game</u> to an even higher level of excellence and helped him defeat his formidable opponent in the Australian Open final yesterday.
這個堅定的信念讓他把比賽表現提升到更高的水準，幫助他在昨天的澳網決賽中擊敗勁敵。

raise + concerns 引起擔憂

That Facebook has access to all of the public information about a user has <u>raised privacy concerns</u>.
Facebook 可以取得用戶的所有公開資訊，此事引起了隱私方面的擔憂。

raise + doubts 引起懷疑

The poll numbers above <u>raise doubts</u>, but let's table that question for the time being.
雖然上述的民調數字令人懷疑，但我們暫時先把這個問題擺一邊。

raise + issue 引出議題、提出問題

On Thursday, Taiwan's representative to the U.S. Hsiao Bi-Khim <u>raised the issue of</u> vaccine availability during a meeting with two U.S. senators.
臺灣駐美代表蕭美琴在週四與兩位美國參議員會面時，提出了疫苗供應的問題。

raise + question 提出問題

The latest issue of the magazine <u>raised the question of</u> when the global chip shortage will end.
最新一期的雜誌提出了全球晶片短缺何時會結束的問題。

raise + money 募款

The NBA player plans to auction a pair of game-worn shoes to <u>raise money for</u> the families of last month's shooting victims.
這位 NBA 球員打算拍賣一雙比賽時穿過的球鞋，為上個月槍擊案的受害者家屬募款。

raise + funds 募集資金

TSMC is keen to <u>raise funds for</u> its production expansion and environmental protection plans from the bond market.
台積電希望從債券市場募集資金，用於擴大產能和環保計畫上。

實用短語 / 用法 / 句型

1. raise the bar 提高標準、門檻

Because so many students are getting good grades on the SAT, universities are <u>raising the bar for</u> students entering their universities.
因為越來越多學生在 SAT 考試中拿到高分，大學正在提高學生的入學門檻。

2. raise eyebrows 令人驚訝、引起反彈

The idea of acquiring the cybersecurity firm <u>raised</u> some <u>eyebrows</u>, but after I went through the details of the plan, board members agreed to support the acquisition.
收購這家網路資安公司的想法引起了些許的反彈，但在我說明了計畫的細節後，董事會成員同意支持這個收購。

3. raise the roof 喧鬧、狂歡

Fans <u>raised the roof</u> on the streets when their team won the championship for the first time in over 60 years.

他們支持的球隊 60 多年來首次贏得冠軍，球迷們在街上喧鬧、狂歡。

Ratify

▶ MP3-107

(ratify — ratified — ratified)

ratify + agreement 批准協議

The teachers union has <u>ratified the agreement</u> earlier in the day. The new agreement, taking effect on July 1, will provide salary increases by 4.3 percent.

教師工會在今天稍早批准了這個協議。新協議將於 7 月 1 日生效，工資將提高 4.3%。

ratify + decision 批准決定

The <u>decision</u> is sure to <u>be ratified</u> by the board on Wednesday.

這個決定肯定會在週三得到董事會的批准。

ratify + treaty 批准條約

Nearly all nations have now <u>ratified the treaty</u>, with the notable exception of the United States.

值得注意的是，除了美國之外，幾乎所有國家都已經批准了這個條約。

Reach

(reach — reached — reached)

reach + agreement 達成協議、達成共識

The two sides <u>reached an agreement on</u> simplifying medical device approval procedures, so people can obtain necessary medical equipment more quickly.
雙方在簡化醫療儀器審查程序上達成共識，讓民眾可以更快速取得必要的醫療設備。

reach + conclusion 得出結論

We believe it is too early to <u>reach a conclusion about</u> how users view this game.
我們認為現在對用戶如何看待這款遊戲下結論還太早。

reach + compromise 達成妥協

She may have the same concerns about the fiscal deficit and may be willing to <u>reach a compromise</u>.
她可能對財政赤字有同樣的擔憂，可能會願意達成妥協。

reach + consensus 達成共識

Perhaps in the near future we can <u>reach a consensus on</u> how to handle these concerns.
或許在不久的將來，我們可以在如何處理這些問題上達成共識。

reach + decision 作出決定

Regulators are scheduled to <u>reach a decision</u> by Feb. 18 <u>on</u> whether they will accept the banks' merger applications.
監管機構預定於 2 月 18 日前決定是否接受兩家銀行的合併申請。

reach + target 達到目標

The latest tightening of regulations is aimed at buying time to <u>reach the target of</u> having two-thirds of the population fully vaccinated by June 1.
近期法規變得更嚴格，目的在於爭取時間，以便在 6 月 1 日前達到讓三分之二的人口完全接種疫苗的目標。

reach + end 到達終點、尾端

It's not all about death. What we do is about helping to make people more comfortable as they <u>reach the end of</u> their lives.
這不僅僅是關於死亡，我們所做的是幫助人們在臨終時能舒服一點。

reach + point 到達～的階段、程度

Parents can <u>reach the point</u> where a child drives them to the end of their patience.
父母可能會被孩子逼到忍無可忍的地步。

reach + level 到達～的程度

To <u>reach the level of</u> skills she has, you must work incredibly hard.
要達到她那樣的能力水準，你必須非常努力。

reach + age 年滿～歲

Employers can compulsorily retire employees who <u>reach the age of</u> 65, provided proper procedures are followed.
只要有遵循適當程序，雇主可以強制年滿 65 歲的員工退休。

實用短語 / 用法 / 句型

1. reach a point of no return 到達無法改變的地步
We should stop the destruction of our natural forests before we <u>reach a point of no return</u>.
在一切都還來得及的時候，我們應該停止對大自然森林的破壞。

Realize

▶ MP3-109

(realize — realized — realized)

realize + dream　實現夢想

He left the company where he had worked for a decade in March 2005 to <u>realize his lifelong dream of</u> starting his own business.

2005 年 3 月，為了實現創業的畢生夢想，他離開了工作 10 年的公司。

realize + goal　實現目標

To help <u>realize that goal</u>, he decided to transfer to a school with a varsity basketball team and scholarship money.

為了幫助實現這個目標，他決定轉到一所擁有籃球校隊並提供獎學金的學校。

realize + idea　實現想法

The focus is on people's needs, combined with the technical possibilities to <u>realize the idea</u> and the economic background, to make your idea a profitable product or service.

重點在於人們的需求，再加上實現想法的技術可行性和經濟背景，來使你的想法成為有獲利能力的產品或服務。

realize + potential 發揮潛力

The top goal of the learning community is to create an educational system where all students can <u>realize their full potential</u>.

學習社群的首要目標是建立一個教育系統，讓所有學生都能充分發揮他們的潛力。

實用短語 / 用法 / 句型

1. one's worst fears are realized 最擔憂、害怕的事情發生

<u>My worst fears were realized</u> when I heard that Jeffery was laid off as part of the merger.

我最擔心的事情還是發生了，我聽說 Jeffery 因為合併案的關係被解僱。

Reap

▶ MP3-110

(reap — reaped — reaped)

reap + benefits 獲得利益、受益

You don't need to be seriously sweating to <u>reap the benefits of</u> regular exercise. Experts say that moderate exercise is enough to help stave off heart disease and other ailments.
你不需要大量流汗來獲得規律運動的好處。專家說，適度的運動就能幫助避免心臟病和其他疾病。

reap + rewards 獲得回報

Lee Chih Kai will <u>reap the rewards of</u> his success as he is set to receive millions after he snatched a silver medal in the Tokyo Olympic Games and became the first Taiwanese Olympic medalist in gymnastics.
李智凱在東京奧運會上奪得銀牌，成為臺灣第一位在奧運體操項目奪牌的選手，他將獲得數百萬元的獎金。

reap + profits 獲利

The private firm is seeking an initial public offering (IPO) in the US to pare debt and <u>reap profits</u> for their investors.
這家私人公司正在美國尋求首次公開募股（IPO），以減少債務並為投資人獲利。

Rebuild

▶ MP3-111

(rebuild — rebuilt — rebuilt)

rebuild + life　重建生活

The organization works to alleviate suffering and to help people <u>rebuild their lives</u> after natural or man-made disasters.

該組織致力於減輕民眾的痛苦，幫助他們在自然或人為災害後重建生活。

rebuild + economy　重振經濟

To help <u>rebuild the</u> American <u>economy</u>, we must directly and effectively help America's small and medium-sized businesses.

為了幫助重建美國經濟，我們必須直接且有效地幫助美國的中小企業。

rebuild + society　重建社會

To <u>rebuild our society</u> and bring back the vibrancy of the economy, the citizens must have a shared vision.

為了重建我們的社會並恢復經濟活力，市民必須有一個共同的願景。

rebuild + home 重建家園

Tens of billions of dollars are expected to be needed to <u>rebuild homes</u>, roads and other infrastructure after the devastating typhoon.

在這個毀滅性的颱風過後，預計需要數百億美元來重建家園、道路和其他基礎建設。

rebuild + trust 重建信任

It's hard to <u>rebuild trust</u> in our relationship after she cheated on me.

在她背叛我之後，我們就很難重建感情中的信任。

Recap

▶ MP3-112

(recap — recapped — recapped)

recap + events　回顧事件

The idea of this program is to <u>recap the major events of</u> the 20th century through the eyes of people who experienced them.

這個節目的想法是，透過經歷過這些事件的人的視角，來回顧 20 世紀的重大事件。

recap + highlights　回顧重點、總結重點

My intent herein is to <u>recap</u> some of <u>the highlights of</u> what such studies should entail and how they should be conducted.

我這裡的目的是總結一些重點，像是這些研究該涵蓋什麼、以及該如何進行。

recap + points　總結要點

At the end of the presentation I will <u>recap the main points</u> and leave some time for the audience to ask questions.

在講座的最後，我會快速總結重點，並留一些時間讓觀眾發問。

Reconcile

▶ MP3-113

(reconcile — reconciled — reconciled)

reconcile + differences 化解分歧、減少差異

While the two parties diverge politically, they should seek communication and dialogue to build up a new model of interaction to <u>reconcile the differences</u>.

即便兩黨在政治立場上分歧，也應尋求溝通與對話，建立新的互動模式，來化解分歧。

reconcile + views 協調觀點

There's a lot of noise around the economic slowdown, and investors are trying to <u>reconcile conflicting views of</u> the market.

關於經濟放緩有諸多雜音，投資人試著對市場的不同觀點做出平衡。

reconcile + needs 協調需求

Turnover is greater among women managers because some of them choose to quit jobs when they cannot <u>reconcile the conflicting needs of</u> work and family.

女性主管的流動率較高，因為有些人在無法兼顧工作與家庭需求時，選擇辭去工作。

Rectify

(rectify — rectified — rectified)

rectify + situation　扭轉局面

In this letter, we apologized and detailed the solutions we took to <u>rectify the situation</u>.

在這封信中，我們道歉並詳細說明我們為了扭轉局面而採取的解決方案。

rectify + problem　糾正問題

You need a long-term solution to <u>rectify the problem of</u> late payment and resurrect your cash flow.

你需要一個長期的解決方案來挽救逾期付款的問題，恢復你的現金流。

rectify + error　糾正錯誤

When we realize that we've sent a message to the wrong person, we normally have a short amount of time to <u>rectify the error</u> before it gets even worse.

當我們發現訊息傳錯人時，通常只有很短的時間來糾正錯誤，以免事情變得更糟。

rectify + damage　彌補傷害

The legislator stressed that her efforts to promote the act aim to <u>rectify the damage of</u> past government policies.

這位立委強調，她努力推動該法案，為的是彌補前政府的政策造成的傷害。

Reduce

▶ MP3-115

(reduce — reduced — reduced)

reduce + risk　降低風險

Maintaining good hand hygiene and cough etiquette helps <u>reduce the risk of</u> becoming infected or spreading infection to others.

維持良好的手部衛生與咳嗽禮節，有助於降低被感染或傳染病毒給他人的風險。

reduce + cost　降低成本

Compared with most other cities in Taiwan, this city has relatively low housing prices, which <u>reduce the cost of</u> living.

與臺灣其他多數的城市相比，這個城市的房價相對較低，進而降低了生活成本。

reduce + number　減少數量

The merger would <u>reduce the number of</u> mobile-phone operators in the U.K. to four.

這併購案使英國的電信業者減少到四家。

reduce + amount　減少數量

I should <u>reduce the amount</u> I spend on streaming services, such as Spotify, Netflix, and Disney Plus.

我應該要減少在串流服務上的花費，像是 Spotify、Netflix、和 Disney+。

reduce + time 減少時間

By scheduling appointments online, you can eliminate the back-and-forth and <u>reduce the time</u> spent on scheduling.
透過上網預約，您可減少往返及花在安排時程上的時間。

reduce + emissions 減少排放量

From a global perspective, the case for a trade tax to <u>reduce</u> CO_2 <u>emissions</u> is weak.
從全球的觀點來看，透過徵收貿易稅來減少二氧化碳排放量的理由不夠充分。

reduce + traffic 減少車流量

The city government urged residents to take advantage of free public transportation services so as to <u>reduce traffic</u> and strengthen environmental protection.
市政府鼓勵民眾利用免費大眾運輸工具，以減少車流量及加強環境保護。

reduce + burden 減輕負擔

We are constantly trying to cut expenses in order to <u>reduce the burden on</u> taxpayers.
我們一直在努力減少支出，以減輕納稅人的負擔。

reduce + pain 減輕疼痛

The studies suggest that these practices appeared to accelerate recovery or <u>reduce pain</u>.
研究指出，這些做法似乎可以加速復原或減輕疼痛。

reduce + stress 減輕壓力

The product manager for lifestyle products has noticed an increase in the number of people shopping for products that claim to <u>reduce stress</u> and depression.
居家生活用品的產品經理注意到，有越來越多人購買聲稱可以減緩壓力或減輕憂鬱情緒的產品。

reduce + need 減少需求

A cutlery set is given to every quarantine guest presented with a set of reusable bowls and plates to <u>reduce the need for</u> disposable utensils.
為減少一次性餐具的需求，每位進行檢疫的客人都會得到一組餐具，內含可重複使用的碗盤。

reduce + impact 減少影響

The Ministry of Transportation and Communications is also making efforts to increase the transport capacity of the Taiwan High Speed Rail and <u>reduce the impact on</u> the environment.
交通部也正努力提高台灣高鐵的可載客量，減少對環境的影響。

reduce + incidence 減少～的發生

He stressed the need to <u>reduce the incidence of</u> unwarranted sick leave if the organization would like to see some changes.
他強調，如果組織希望看到一些改變，就必須減少無故請病假的狀況發生。

reduce + likelihood 減少可能性

Boards usually have an odd number of members to <u>reduce the likelihood of</u> a tie vote.
董事會成員人數通常是奇數，以減少票數平手的可能性。

reduce + chance 減少機會

If drivers used snow chains, they would greatly <u>reduce the chance of</u> accidents and damage.
如果駕駛人使用雪鏈，他們會大大減少事故發生和車輛損壞的機會。

reduce + possibility 減少可能性

After certain confidential employee information was acquired without authorization, we are now analyzing our systems to <u>reduce the possibility of</u> any future breaches.
某些機密的員工資料在未經授權的狀況下被取得後，我們正在分析系統，以減少未來任何違法行為發生的可能性。

reduce + potential 降低潛在性

If done correctly, the process should strengthen market discipline on banks and <u>reduce the potential for</u> systemic risk.

如果執行得當，這個流程應可強化銀行的市場紀律，並降低潛在的系統風險。

reduce + use 減少～的使用

Regulators must be able to step in and <u>reduce the use of</u> leverage in any financial market that starts to get frothy.

在任何開始出現泡沫化的金融市場中，監管機構必須能夠介入並減少槓桿的使用。

reduce + price 降低價格

Tesla cut 7 percent of its workforce last month to trim costs and <u>reduce the price of</u> the car.

特斯拉上個月裁員 7%，以節省成本、降低這款車的售價。

reduce + reliance 減少對～的依賴

Japan's new leader has promised to <u>reduce reliance on</u> debt financing and release a plan in June.

日本新任首相承諾，將減少對債務融資的依賴，並在 6 月公布計畫。

Refine

(refine — refined — refined)

refine + search 改善、優化搜尋

You may need to <u>refine your search</u> to locate information you are seeking.
你可能需要優化搜尋來找到你要的資訊。

refine + quality 改善品質

This winery's next challenge is to <u>refine the quality of</u> its wines to be on par with famous overseas regions.
這個酒莊的下一個挑戰是，如何將葡萄酒的品質提高到與海外著名產地相同的水準。

refine + results 改善、優化結果

Using quotation marks may be beneficial to <u>refine search results</u>. This helps to narrow down the results and save you time.
使用引號可能有助於優化搜尋結果。這會幫助縮小搜尋結果的範圍並節省你的時間。

refine + design 改善設計

To <u>refine the design</u>, we must model and analyze the proposed design whenever possible.
為了改善設計，我們必須盡可能把提出的設計做建模與分析。

Relax

▶ MP3-117

(relax — relaxed — relaxed)

relax + restrictions 放寬限制

The Ministry of Health and Welfare plans to extend the nationwide Level 3 COVID-19 alert, as the disease still poses a risk to the community, but said it will <u>relax restrictions on</u> daily and social activities.
由於新冠病毒對社區仍構成威脅，衛福部計劃將延長全國疫情第三級警戒，但將放寬對日常生活及社交活動的限制。

relax + rules 放寬規定

Voters were divided on whether to <u>relax rules on</u> environmental reviews of developments.
對於是否放寬開發項目的環境評估規定，選民意見不一。

relax + requirement 放寬規定、要求

The changes also will <u>relax existing requirements for</u> providing foreign workers housing and transportation.
這些改變也將放寬對外籍勞工提供住房及交通的現行規定。

relax + controls 放寬管制

China has always aimed to increase imports from the U.S. and hopes the U.S. can do more to <u>relax export controls</u>.
中國一直致力於增加從美國進口的商品，希望美國可以進一步放寬出口管制。

relax + regulations 放寬規定

Health officials are planning to <u>relax regulations on</u> mandatory quarantine for arrivals.
衛生官員正計劃放寬入境旅客強制隔離的規定。

relax + muscles 放鬆肌肉

Going back and forth from cold to warm is supposed to improve circulation and <u>relax your muscles</u>.
冷熱交替可以改善血液循環、放鬆肌肉。

relax + body 放鬆身體

Laughter helps <u>relax your body</u> and provides a nice distraction from all the stressful things going on in your life.
笑有助於放鬆你的身體，讓你忘記生活中的壓力。

relax + mind 放鬆心情

Turn off your mobile device for some time each day. Just get away from it to <u>relax your mind</u>.
每天把你的行動裝置關掉一段時間。遠離它來放鬆心情。

Release

▶ MP3-118

(release — released — released)

release + information 發布消息、公布資訊

The former president argued that the government should
<u>release information about</u> its vaccine procurement budget.
前總統認為政府應該公布疫苗採購預算的資訊。

release + statement 發表聲明

The Chinese embassy in the U.K. <u>released a statement</u>
on Aug. 1, expressing its extreme dissatisfaction over the
BBC's Taiwan-related coverage of the Tokyo Olympics.
中國駐英大使館 8 月 1 日發表聲明，針對英國廣播公司關於東京奧
運會的臺灣相關報導表達強烈不滿。

release + report 發布報告

The bureau <u>released a report</u> after torrential rains caused
serious flooding. It called for improved rainwater drainage
systems along major roads.
在暴雨造成嚴重水災後，該局發布了一份報告。它呼籲改善主要道
路的雨水下水道系統。

release + data 公布數據

A private research group <u>released data</u> on Tuesday
showing consumer confidence moved higher in May.
一個民間研究團隊週二公布了數據，顯示 5 月的消費者信心有所提升。

release + results 公布結果

The <u>results released</u> last Friday beat expectations as the company's business improved. Its stock rose 2.6 percent in trading Monday.

隨著公司業績提升，上週五公布的結果超越預期。其股價在週一交易中上漲了 2.6%。

release + album 發行專輯

This South Korean band <u>released its</u> second <u>album</u> in May and returned to No. 1 on Billboard.

這個南韓團體 5 月發行了第二張專輯，重返告示牌專輯榜第一名。

release + film 上映電影

The first <u>film</u> in the series, <u>released</u> in 2001, had been a surprise hit, making $206 million worldwide.

這個系列的第一部電影在 2001 年上映，非常成功，全球票房達 2 億 6 百萬美元。

release + video 發布影片

The former president has <u>released a</u> YouTube <u>video</u> previewing his upcoming book.

前總統在 YouTube 上發布了新影片，預告他即將出版的新書。

Relieve

▶ MP3-119

(relieve — relieved — relieved)

relieve + pain 緩解疼痛

The goal is not only to <u>relieve pain</u> but also, possibly, to halt progression of the disease.
目標不僅是要緩解疼痛，可能的話，還要阻止疾病惡化。

relieve + symptoms 緩解症狀

These drugs can all <u>relieve symptoms</u>, but adverse effects are common with all of them.
這些藥物都能緩解症狀，但也常有副作用。

relieve + anxiety 緩解焦慮

Writing down tasks for the day helps to focus my mind and <u>relieve anxiety</u>.
寫下當天的工作可以幫助我集中注意力並緩解焦慮。

relieve + suffering 減輕痛苦

A panel of experts will work with the council to build on existing courses of treatment and develop new ones to <u>relieve</u> patients' <u>suffering</u>.
專家小組將與委員會合作，在現有療法的基礎上研發新的療法，以減輕患者痛苦。

relieve + stress 緩解壓力

Yoga is often recommended to heart and cancer patients as a way to <u>relieve stress</u>.
瑜伽經常被推薦給心臟病和癌症患者，作為一種緩解壓力的方法。

relieve + pressure 減緩壓力

In the face of that emergency, doctors should have inserted a needle into the lungs to <u>relieve the pressure</u>.
面對這種緊急情況，醫生應該將針刺入肺部來減緩壓力。

relieve + tension 緩解緊張、壓力

Why not treat yourself to a fancy steak dinner to <u>relieve tension</u> at the close of the work week?
為什麼不在工作週結束後，吃一頓美味的牛排當晚餐來紓解壓力呢？

relieve + discomfort 緩解不適

Is laser treatment a viable possibility? We would be happy to learn more about any treatments to <u>relieve his discomfort</u>.
雷射治療可行嗎？我們很樂意了解更多治療方案來緩解他的不適。

relieve + boredom 排解無聊、解悶

I had thought that watching a series on Netflix could be a good way to take my mind off things and <u>relieve the boredom</u>, but I couldn't help thinking about her.
我原以為在 Netflix 上看影集是個很好的方式來轉移我的注意力、排解無聊,但我還是忍不住想起她。

relieve + congestion 緩解壅塞

To <u>relieve congestion</u>, construction on a new interchange is slated to start in the spring.
為了緩解壅塞,新的交流道預計將於今年春天開工。

relieve + burden 減輕負擔

To <u>relieve the burden on</u> local healthcare facilities, we are sending extra doctors and nurses to these areas
為了減輕當地醫療機構的負擔,我們正向這些地區增派醫生和護士。

relieve + itching 止癢

You can <u>relieve itching</u> and reduce the risk of skin damage caused by scratching with some simple measures.
你可以利用一些簡單的方法來止癢,減少抓到破皮的風險。

Repair

(repair — repaired — repaired)

---

repair + damage 彌補傷害、修復損害

It may not be possible to <u>repair the damage</u> I've done, but I want to do my best to try.
雖然可能無法彌補我造成的傷害，但我想盡最大的努力試試。

---

repair + problem 修復問題

This position must be able to <u>repair problems</u> in a timely manner.
這個職位必須要能夠即時修復問題。

---

repair + defect 修復瑕疵、缺陷

Our engineer will <u>repair the defect</u> as described by the customer. The product will also be tested to ensure it is working properly.
我們的工程師將依照客戶的描述修復瑕疵。這個產品也將進行測試，以確保它能正常運作。

---

repair + product 維修產品

If your product is still within the standard warranty, ASUS will, at its option, <u>repair</u> or replace <u>the product</u>.
如果您的產品仍在標準保固內，華碩將依據檢測結果維修或更換產品。

repair + equipment 維修設備

The lack of rain allows the division more time to <u>repair equipment</u> needed for construction season.

因為沒有下雨，使該部門有更多時間維修施工季所需的設備。

repair + relationship 修復關係

Total honesty is the key to <u>repairing relationship</u> after cheating.

完全誠實是出軌後要修復關係的關鍵。

Repel

▶ MP3-121

(repel — repelled — repelled)

repel + attack 擊退進攻

Ukrainian soldiers were trying to <u>repel</u> Russian <u>attacks</u> and casualties were mounting.
烏克蘭士兵試圖擊退俄羅斯的進攻，傷亡人數不斷增加。

repel + invaders 擊退入侵者

The general used all kinds of ingenious and creative tactics to <u>repel the invaders</u>.
將軍運用各種巧妙有創意的策略擊退入侵者。

repel + enemy 擊退敵人

The law criminalizes the use of the military unless it is necessary to <u>repel</u> armed <u>enemies</u>.
法律規定，除非有必要擊退武裝敵人，否則使用軍隊是犯法的。

Resolve

(resolve — resolved — resolved)

resolve + problem 解決問題

U.S. senators asked the Taiwanese government to help address the chip shortage, given that the country is a major semiconductor producer and seen as central to efforts to <u>resolve the problem</u>.

因為臺灣是主要的半導體生產國,並被視為解決問題的核心角色, 美國參議員要求臺灣政府幫助解決晶片短缺的問題。

resolve + issue 解決問題

North Korea's leader said that he is willing to resume talks to <u>resolve the issue of</u> nuclear weapons.

北韓領導人表示,他願意恢復會談,以解決核武問題。

resolve + matter 解決事情

The authority hopes to <u>resolve the matter</u> within a couple of weeks and doesn't expect any delays in construction.

當局希望在幾週內解決此事,不希望工程有任何延誤。

resolve + situation 解決情況

This is a private matter, which has no impact on the day-to-day operations of business. We are doing all we can to <u>resolve the situation</u> privately.
這是私事，對公司的日常營運沒有影響。我們正在盡我們所能私下解決這個情況。

resolve + dispute 解決紛爭、爭議

A meeting is scheduled today between representatives from both parties to try to <u>resolve the dispute</u> over abortion.
兩黨代表訂於今天舉行會議，試圖解決墮胎的爭議。

resolve + conflict 解決衝突

What do you think the next President has to do to <u>resolve the</u> Israeli-Palestinian <u>conflict</u>?
你認為下一任總統應該如何解決以巴衝突？

resolve + crisis 解決危機

We hope stricter rules will not only <u>resolve the crisis</u> but ensure it does not recur.
我們希望更嚴格的規定不僅能解決危機，也能確保它不會再次發生。

resolve + differences 解決分歧

A hearing scheduled for next month is unlikely to <u>resolve differences between</u> the opposing sides.
訂於下個月舉行的聽證會不太可能解決對立雙方的分歧。

resolve + complaint 解決抱怨、投訴

Strong communication skills are needed to meet client needs and <u>resolve complaints</u>.
要滿足客戶需求和解決投訴，需要具備出色的溝通能力。

Retain

▶ MP3-123

(retain — retained — retained)

retain + right 保留權利

The photographer who did our family portrait wants to <u>retain the right</u> to use the photos to promote their business.
幫我們拍全家福照的攝影師希望能保留使用照片的權利，來宣傳他們的業務。

retain + control 保留對～的控制

The bank will <u>retain control of</u> the company until the loans are repaid.
在貸款還清之前，銀行將繼續掌管這間公司。

retain + moisture 保濕、保留水分

This lotion can help your skin <u>retain moisture</u> and inhibit oil production.
這款乳液可以幫助你的皮膚保濕並抑制油脂分泌。

retain + customers 留住顧客

Many companies strive to maintain customer loyalty because it's cheaper to <u>retain customers</u> than to acquire new ones.
許多公司努力維持顧客忠誠度，因為留住顧客比招攬新顧客的成本更低。

Reveal

▶ MP3-124

(reveal — revealed — revealed)

reveal + information 透露、揭露資訊

The law obliges large companies to <u>reveal information</u> on a public website <u>about</u> their supply chain.
該法要求大型公司在公開網站上揭露有關其供應鏈的資訊。

reveal + truth 揭露事實、真相

People hit the streets and continued to demand that the authorities <u>reveal the truth</u> behind this case.
人們走上街頭，持續要求當局揭露這起事件背後的真相。

reveal + secret 洩密

Weak privacy protection can <u>reveal</u> business <u>secrets</u> to people who should not know about the company's internal matters, thus resulting in severe business loss.
薄弱的隱私保護可能將商業機密洩露給不應該知道公司內部事務的人，進而造成嚴重的業務損失。

A
B
C
D
E
F
G
H
I
J
K
L
M
N
O
P
Q
R
S
T
U
V
W

reveal + details 透露細節

The mayor was unable to <u>reveal details about</u> the program at a press conference Thursday but said the vouchers will be spendable at traditional markets, night markets, and hotels.
市長無法在週四的記者會上透露關於該計畫的細節，但表示這些抵用券可用於傳統市場、夜市和飯店。

reveal + identity 揭露身分

A police officer confirmed that the stolen car was recovered a short time later, but did not <u>reveal the identity of</u> the owner.
一名員警證實，失竊的車輛很快就找到了，但並沒有透露車主的身分。

reveal + contents 透露～的內容

He declined to <u>reveal the contents of</u> the letter, except to say it includes a recommendation and alternatives.
他拒絕透露這封信的內容，只表示信中包含一項建議和替代方案。

reveal + answer 揭曉答案

What happens when you mix doses of the Pfizer and AstraZeneca vaccines? A new study <u>reveals the answer</u>, saying receiving a second dose of a different vaccine might produce a stronger immune response.
混打輝瑞和 AZ 的疫苗會怎麼樣？一項新研究揭曉答案，聲稱第二劑接種不同廠牌的疫苗可能產生更強的免疫反應。

Revise

▶ MP3-125

(revise — revised — revised)

---

revise + terms 修改條款

You can <u>revise the terms of</u> use when there is a change in the conditions that your customer must comply with.
當客戶必須遵守的條件改變時，你可以修改使用條款。

---

revise + plan 修改計畫

The group will reconvene the following Monday to figure out what worked and what didn't, and to <u>revise the plan</u>.
團隊將在下週一重新召開會議，以確定哪些計畫可行、哪些無效，並做修改。

---

revise + draft 修改草稿

The writing consultant usually responds to the student's concerns first, then works with the student to plan other ways to <u>revise the draft</u>.
寫作顧問通常會先回答學生的問題，然後與學生一起想其他方式來修改草稿。

revise + paper　修改論文

We have carefully considered your comments as well as those offered by three reviewers. Herein, we explain how we <u>revised the paper</u> based on those comments and recommendations.

我們仔細考量了您以及三位評審的意見，在此說明我們是如何根據這些意見和建議修改論文的。

revise + search　修改搜尋

If the search results list seems too large or too broad, you can <u>revise your search</u> to narrow it down.

如果搜尋結果列表看起來太多或太廣，你可以修改搜尋以縮小範圍。

revise + proposal　修改提案

I was wondering if I could <u>revise the proposal</u> and address all identified weaknesses before the deadline.

不知道我是否可以在截止日前修改提案、並解決所有確定不足的地方。

revise + budget　修改預算

Government officials announced they would <u>revise the budget</u> to take into account falling oil prices and shrinking credit markets.

政府官員宣布，為考量油價下跌及信貸市場萎縮，他們將修改預算。

Revitalize

▶ MP3-126

(revitalize — revitalized — revitalized)

revitalize + economy　振興經濟

Another question is whether the government will be able to recoup the money it is spending to revitalize the economy.
另一個問題是，政府是否能收回為了振興經濟所投入的資金。

revitalize + skin　使皮膚恢復活力

The company says the Chinese herbal extracts naturally cleanse and revitalize skin without drying it out.
該公司表示，這種中藥萃取物可以自然淨化肌膚，並使肌膚恢復活力，而不會造成皮膚乾燥。

revitalize + company　重振公司

To revitalize the company, he has sold off unprofitable plants and cut staff.
為了重振公司，他賣掉虧錢的工廠並裁員。

revitalize + industry　重振產業

If the candidate can revitalize the auto industry, could that create more employment opportunities?
如果這位候選人能夠重振汽車產業，這是否會創造更多的就業機會？

Ruin

(ruin — ruined — ruined)

ruin + life 毀掉生活

The actress tried to <u>ruin</u> her ex-husband's <u>life</u> by accusing him of domestic violence.
這位女演員試圖透過控告前夫家暴，來毀掉他的生活。

ruin + career 毀掉職業生涯

He suggested that the video was leaked intentionally to <u>ruin her career</u>.
他表示這段影片是故意外流的，目的是要毀掉她的職業生涯。

ruin + chance 毀掉機會

That was a costly turnover and almost <u>ruined their chances of</u> winning the championship.
那個失誤的代價非常高，差點毀了他們奪冠的機會。

ruin + surprise 毀了驚喜

I don't want to <u>ruin the surprise</u>, but since you're interested, there may be something you can help me with.
我不想破壞驚喜，但既然你有興趣，也許你能幫我些什麼。

ruin + fun 破壞樂趣

There is a method to win the game, but if I tell you now, it'll <u>ruin the fun</u>.
有一個方法可以贏得遊戲，但如果我現在告訴你，那會破壞樂趣。

ruin + experience 毀了體驗

Our unique dining <u>experience was ruined</u> by the actions of a small number of very selfish people.
我們獨特的用餐體驗被少數非常自私的個人行為毀了。

ruin + trip 毀了旅程

Contracting COVID-19 <u>ruined her trip to</u> the U.S. and had major consequences on her health.
感染 COVID-19 毀了她的美國之旅，並對她的健康造成嚴重影響。

ruin + reputation 毀了名聲

One mistake can <u>ruin</u> a brand's <u>reputation</u> and destroy its trust with consumers.
一個錯誤就能毀掉一個品牌的聲譽和消費者對它的信任。

ruin + mood 破壞心情

I don't want to <u>ruin the mood</u> for everyone, but the last thing I want now is to think about the party.
我不想破壞大家的心情，但我現在最不想做的就是想派對的事情。

Run

(run — ran — run)

run + risk 冒險、面臨風險

We'd better attend the meeting tomorrow. We don't want to
<u>run the risk of</u> losing our business.
我們最好要參加明天的會議。我們不想冒會失去生意的風險。

run + errands 跑腿、辦事情

If you're very busy, you may need someone to <u>run errands</u>
or help with mailings.
如果你很忙，你可能需要有人幫忙跑腿或幫忙寄信。

run + gamut 涵蓋全部範圍、所有領域

The tech company's products <u>run the gamut</u> from home
appliances to computer modules for electric vehicles.
這家科技公司的產品涵蓋了從家電到電動汽車的電腦模組等各個領域。

run + test 進行測試

To export their cars, automakers must <u>run the test</u> again to
meet other governments' measurement standards.
為了出口汽車，汽車製造商必須再次進行測試，以滿足其他國家的
測量標準。

run + check 進行檢查

Credit card providers <u>run a check on</u> an individual's credit file when assessing an application.
信用卡公司在評估申請時，會檢查個人的信用紀錄。

run + course 開設課程

For each course, the group size will be 16 people maximum. We will need a minimum of six people in order to <u>run the course</u>.
每門課程最多可以收 16 人。而我們至少需要 6 個人才能開設這門課。

run + business 經營公司；經營生意

The financial regulator is scheduled to issue the first batch of licenses to companies applying for permission to <u>run the business</u> in Taiwan.
金融監管機構計劃核發第一批許可證，給申請在臺灣經營業務的公司。

run + company 經營公司

My job is to <u>run the company</u> and continue to get value for customers and shareholders.
我的工作是經營公司並繼續為客戶和股東創造價值。

run + fever　發燒

After <u>running a fever</u> for days, she sought care at a local hospital and was tested for COVID-19 on April 6.

在發燒幾天後，她前往當地一家醫院就醫，並於 4 月 6 日接受 COVID-19 檢測。

run + red light　闖紅燈

He and two friends were killed after their car was hit by a van that <u>ran a red light</u>.

他和兩名朋友被一輛闖紅燈的貨車撞死。

實用短語 / 用法 / 句型

1. run a tight ship　嚴格管理

She <u>runs a tight ship</u> and her kids can't snack until they have done their homework.

她管得很嚴，她的孩子在完成作業前都不能吃零食。

2. run for office　參選

Civil groups called for election deposits to be abolished, to ensure that everyone has an equal right to <u>run for office</u>.

民間團體呼籲廢除選舉保證金，以確保每個人都有平等的參選權利。

3. run its course 順其自然

Unfortunately, there's no treatment for this kind of infection. What you can do is let it <u>run its course</u>.
不幸的是，這種感染沒有方法可以治療。你能做的就是讓它自然好起來。

4. run before sb can walk 還不會走就想飛、好高騖遠

As an English teacher, I've seen a lot of students who want to <u>run before they can walk</u>.
身為一位英文老師，我見過很多好高騖遠的學生。

Scratch

(scratch — scratched — scratched)

scratch + plan 取消計畫

Last year, Facebook showed interest in building a data center with an approximately US$309 million investment in Changhua, but the social media company later <u>scratched the plan</u>.

Facebook 去年表示，有興趣在彰化投資約 3.09 億美元打造一個資料數據中心，但後來取消了這個計畫。

實用短語 / 用法 / 句型

1. scratch one's head 苦思

I've heard this question a couple of times lately and the very premise of it made me <u>scratch my head</u>.

我最近已經聽到這個問題好幾次，它的前提假設讓我苦思了很久。

2. scratch the surface 觸及事情、問題的表面

The council have managed to provide housing for over ten thousand homeless people but they say they have only <u>scratched the surface of</u> the problem.

委員會已經想辦法為超過一萬名無家可歸者提供住所，但他們說這只觸及了問題的表面。

3. scratch beneath the surface 深入了解、剖析

The film presents a few interesting ideas, but it fails to <u>scratch beneath the surface</u> with any of them.

這部電影呈現了一些有趣的點，但沒有深入剖析任何一個面向。

4. scratch out a living 勉強維生

These migrant workers <u>scratch out a living</u> by working at least 12 hours a day in unsafe conditions.

這些外籍勞工每天要在不安全的環境下工作至少 12 個小時才能勉強維生。

Seal

(seal — sealed — sealed)

seal + agreement 達成協議

The sale of arms is temporarily put on hold, although the officials are confident it will go through once the U.S. and China <u>seal an agreement</u>.

軍售案暫時被擱置，不過官員們有信心，一旦美國和中國達成協議，軍售將獲得批准。

seal + deal 達成協議、交易

Today's meeting may open the door for our business, but following up will help <u>seal the deal</u>.

今天這場會議可以為我們的業務打開大門、帶來機會，但後續的工作才有助於搞定這筆生意。

seal + win 鎖定勝利

He hit four consecutive free throws and a late 3-pointer to help <u>seal the win</u>.

他連續投進四顆罰球以及一顆絕殺三分球，幫助球隊鎖定勝利。

seal + victory 鎖定勝利

In the second half, Italy topped Germany 92-82, including a 12-0 to <u>seal the victory</u> and end the game.

下半場，義大利以 92-82 擊敗德國，其中一波 12-0 的攻勢鎖定了勝利並結束比賽。

seal + game 鎖定勝利

Kyrie Irving helped <u>seal the game</u> in the fourth quarter with his continuous drives. He finished with 34 points, five assists and just three turnovers.

Kyrie Irving 在第四節藉著連續幾波進攻鎖定了勝利。他最終拿下 34 分、5 次助攻、僅有 3 次失誤。

實用短語 / 用法 / 句型

1. seal one's fate 決定某人的命運

If you fail this exam, it will <u>seal your fate</u> and make your GPA low enough to qualify for expulsion.

如果你這次考試不及格，就注定了你的學科成績會低到要被退學。

Settle

▶ MP3-131

(settle — settled — settled)

settle + dispute 解決紛爭、爭議

The Minister said that Beijing's ban on imports of fruit from Taiwan was unacceptable, vowing to <u>settle the dispute</u> through the WTO if Beijing continues to ignore requests for trade negotiations.

部長表示對於北京禁止臺灣水果進口是無法接受的，並誓言如果北京繼續無視貿易談判的要求，將透過世界貿易組織解決此紛爭。

settle + argument 解決爭論

These insights do not, however, <u>settle the argument over</u> what role the government should play in nurturing the young.

然而，這些見解並沒有解決政府在培養年輕人方面應該扮演何種角色的爭論。

settle + conflict 解決衝突

Despite many years of effort, we still don't see a future where the <u>conflict</u> between the two arch-rivals <u>is settled</u>.

即便經過多年的努力，這兩個死對頭間的衝突在未來仍難化解。

settle + differences 解決分歧

After a long battle, the two companies have finally <u>settled their differences</u>. They are now working together to incorporate augmented reality into future smartphone applications.

經過長期的鬥爭，這兩家公司終於解決了分歧。他們正在合作，要將擴增虛擬實境的技術，整合到未來的智慧型手機應用程式中。

settle + issue 解決問題

New Education Minister said he met with the convener of the National Taiwan University presidential selection committee for an hour and proposed ways to <u>settle the issue</u>.

新任教育部長表示，他與臺大校長遴選委員會召集人進行了一個小時的會談，並提出問題的解決方案。

settle + problem 解決問題

She apologized for what had happened and wrote a check in the amount of $300, hoping to <u>settle the problem</u>.

她為發生的事情道歉，並開了一張 300 美元的支票，希望能解決這個問題。

settle + question 解決問題

In the past few years, some well-designed studies have <u>settled the question of</u> whether muscle strength has anything to do with living longer.

在過去幾年裡，一些經過縝密設計的研究，已經解決了肌肉強度是否與長壽有關的問題。

settle + date 確定日期

Could we <u>settle the date of</u> this meeting when we know more details?

能否等我們知道更多的細節後，再來確定這次會議的日期？

settle + details 確定細節

<u>Details</u> of the plan remain to <u>be settled</u>, but the idea is that transport, energy and industry will be included.

該計畫的細節尚待確定，但想法是運輸、能源和工業會被包括在內。

Snatch

▶ MP3-132

(snatch — snatched — snatched)

snatch + lead 取得領先

It was 50-43 at the half. The Celtics finally <u>snatched the lead</u> early in the third quarter by scoring nine straight points.
上半場比分為 50-43，塞爾提克隊終於在第三節開始的時候連拿 9 分取得領先。

snatch + victory 取得勝利

The candidate <u>snatched victory</u> in last year's general election by claiming refugees as a threat to security.
這位候選人主張難民會對安全造成威脅，進而在去年的大選中獲得勝利。

snatch + medal 奪得獎牌

Team USA <u>snatched a</u> fourth straight Olympic <u>gold medal</u> as they beat France 87-82 in Tokyo.
美國隊在東奧以 87-82 擊敗法國隊，連續四次奪得奧運金牌。

A
B
C
D
E
F
G
H
I
J
K
L
M
N
O
P
Q
R
S
T
U
V
W

實用短語 / 用法 / 句型

1. snatch from one's grasp 從某人手中奪走

Derek Fisher scored to make it 74-73 and <u>snatched</u> <u>victory from</u> the Spurs' <u>grasp</u>.

Derek Fisher 投進並將比分改寫為 74-73，從馬刺隊手中奪走勝利。

Soothe

▶ MP3-133

(soothe — soothed — soothed)

soothe + pain 緩解疼痛

He went into the doctor's office for his sore back, hoping to be prescribed some medicine to <u>soothe the pain</u>.
他因為背痛去看醫生，希望能拿一些藥緩解疼痛。

soothe + nerves 緩解緊張

To <u>soothe nerves</u>, the Bank of Japan injected about $22 billion into banks and other financial institutions.
為了安撫緊張情緒，日本央行出手向銀行及其他金融機構注入約 220 億美元。

soothe + soul 撫慰心靈、療癒心靈

If you're struggling with anxiety and stress, here are 10 ways to <u>soothe your soul</u>.
如果你正面臨焦慮和壓力，這裡有 10 種方法可以撫慰你的心靈。

soothe + skin 舒緩肌膚

Nowadays there are various products available that both moisturize and <u>soothe the skin</u>, helping to prevent irritation following a shave.
現在有各式產品可以滋潤和舒緩肌膚，有助於預防刮鬍後的不適。

soothe + throat 舒緩喉嚨

A lot of people advocate drinking tea to <u>soothe your sore throat</u> or any other symptoms that you have.
很多人提倡喝茶來舒緩喉嚨痛或其他症狀。

soothe + muscles 舒緩肌肉

Try these five simple tips to <u>soothe sore muscles</u> and speed up your post-workout recovery.
試試這五個簡單的方法來舒緩肌肉酸痛並加速運動後的恢復。

Spare

▶ MP3-134

(spare — spared — spared)

spare + time 抽出時間

Two-thirds of the nurses said they were unable to <u>spare the time</u> while working to get a drink of water.
有三分之二的護理師表示，他們在工作時抽不出時間喝水。

實用短語 / 用法 / 句型

1. spare no effort 不遺餘力、全力以赴

Taipei 101 stated that it will continue to implement the highest standards of epidemic prevention measures and <u>spare no effort to</u> maintain the health and safety of employees and customers.
台北 101 表示，將持續實施最高標準的防疫措施，全力維護員工和顧客的健康與安全。

2. spare no expense 不惜成本、全力以赴

Many K-pop fans <u>spare no expense to</u> purchase merchandise to get closer to their favorite pop stars.
許多韓國流行音樂的粉絲不惜成本購買商品，來更接近自己喜愛的歌手。

3. spare a thought for sb 替某人想想、想想某人

When you're complaining, <u>spare a thought for</u> those who are less fortunate than you.
當你在抱怨的時候，想想那些比你不幸的人吧。

Spark

▶ MP3-135

(spark — sparked — sparked)

spark + interest 引起、激發興趣

The president called for more cooperation between industry, academia, and government to <u>spark interest in</u> scientific research among outstanding young students.
總統呼籲產業界、學術界和政府之間有更多的合作，以激發優秀年輕學子對科學研究的興趣。

spark + debate 引發爭論

The critic's remarks <u>sparked debate about</u> whether this player's Finals MVP is well deserved.
這位球評的言論，引發了關於這位球員的總決賽最有價值球員獎是否實至名歸的爭論。

spark + discussion 引發討論

The idea of this event is to get people reading and <u>spark discussion about</u> the book and an interest in the issue of migrant workers.
這個活動的想法是促進民眾閱讀，進而引發對這本書的討論，以及對移工問題的興趣。

spark + imagination 引發、激發想像

Interactive games and do-it-yourself experiences offered in the exhibition can <u>spark the imagination</u> and creativity <u>of</u> teachers and students.
展覽提供的互動式遊戲和 DIY 體驗可以激發師生的想像力及創造力。

spark + controversy 引起爭議

Some of the management changes <u>sparked controversy</u> before they were formally announced.
管理階層的一些變動在正式宣布之前就引起了爭議。

Stir

(stir — stirred — stirred)

stir + imagination 激發想像

The company just came into existence this year and has
stirred the imagination of cryptocurrency fans.
這間公司今年剛剛成立，激發了加密貨幣粉絲的想像。

stir + emotions 激起、煽動情緒

The image of a dead Syrian child washed up on a beach
really stirred up our emotions.
一名敘利亞孩童的屍體被沖上海灘的畫面激起了我們的情緒。

stir + memories 喚起回憶

Seeing this old house stirs our memories of family
celebrations, loved ones and the everyday pleasures of
times past.
看到這間老房子，喚起我們對家庭慶祝活動、親人、以及過去日常
快樂的回憶。

stir + curiosity 引起好奇心

I'm not usually one to seek out a show full of newbie actors,
but your positive comments on this drama have stirred my
curiosity.
我通常不喜歡看有很多新演員的劇，但你對這部劇的好評引起了我
的好奇心。

Strengthen

▶ MP3-137

(strengthen — strengthened — strengthened)

---

strengthen + capacity 加強能力

The goal is to establish global banking regulations to strengthen the capacity of banks to withstand a future crisis.
目標是建立全球銀行業的規範,以加強銀行抵禦未來危機的能力。

---

strengthen + position 強化地位

Google announced two big deals to strengthen its position as the market leader in online advertising.
Google 宣布了兩項重大交易,以強化其網路廣告市場領導者的地位。

---

strengthen + ties 強化關係

Japan wants to strengthen ties with the central European leaders and boost investment to catch up with China.
日本希望強化與中歐領導人的關係,並擴大投資來趕上中國。

---

strengthen + relationship 強化關係

The official wants to help strengthen the financial relationship between Hong Kong and mainland China and promote globalization of the yuan.
新任官員希望協助強化香港與中國大陸之間的金融關係,推動人民幣國際化。

strengthen + links 強化關係

As businesses look to expand and <u>strengthen their links</u> across national borders, professionals with experience of a multiplicity of variant business cultures will be in increased demand.

因為企業希望擴大和加強跨國關係，具有多元商業文化經驗的專業人才的需求將會增加。

strengthen + bonds 強化關係

The event was a chance to <u>strengthen bonds</u> within the community and give children and adults the opportunity to mix.

這活動是個強化社區關係的機會，也讓小孩和成人有機會交流。

strengthen + economy 強化經濟

The Fed's $600 billion Treasury bond-buying program is ending this month. The program was intended to keep interest rates low to <u>strengthen the economy</u>.

美國聯準會 6,000 億美元的購債計畫將在這個月結束。這計畫的目的是維持低利率來強化經濟。

strengthen + efforts 加強力道、努力

An overall development plan for the old town, beyond the scheme's immediate focus on housing, could <u>strengthen efforts</u> further.

除了立即關注住房問題外，舊城區的整體發展計畫可能還需要再更努力。

Stretch

▶ MP3-138

(stretch — stretched — stretched)

stretch + truth 誇大事實

Startup founders are apt to exaggerate and <u>stretch the truth</u> when courting investors and other important stakeholders.
新創公司創辦人在討好投資人和其他重要股東時，往往會誇大事實。

stretch + boundaries 突破界限

People who aren't afraid to be different naturally <u>stretch boundaries</u> and challenge the status quo, and they often come up with the best ideas.
不害怕與眾不同的人自然會突破極限、挑戰現狀，而他們往往能想出最好的主意。

stretch + limits 突破極限

In Taiwan, industry giants are embracing the cloud to <u>stretch the limits of</u> what's possible when teams work together with technology.
在臺灣，產業巨頭漸漸擁抱雲端技術，以擴展團隊與科技結合帶來的可能性。

stretch + imagination 超乎想像

It does not <u>stretch the imagination</u> to appreciate that a warmer atmosphere promotes greater melting of the polar ice caps, thereby raising sea levels .

不難想像,暖化的氣候會加速極地冰帽融化,進而導致海平面上升。

stretch + budget 把預算的效益最大化、做最好的運用

All of the guidebooks that are about saving money are really geared towards backpackers. For example, many of them suggest that travelers stay in hostels to help <u>stretch their budget</u>.

所有的省錢指南都是為背包客設計的。例如,很多指南會建議背包客住青年旅館,來將預算做最好的運用。

stretch + rules 通融

We don't normally employ people over 50, but in your case we're prepared to <u>stretch the rules</u> a little.

我們通常不會僱用 50 歲以上的員工,但對於你的情況,我們會稍做通融。

stretch + lead 擴大領先

The Cavaliers hit four three-pointers in a row to <u>stretch the lead to</u> 13 at one point.

騎士隊連續投進四個三分球,一度將領先優勢擴大到 13 分。

Tackle

▶ MP3-139

(tackle — tackled — tackled)

tackle + problem　解決問題

Free shipping is one way to <u>tackle the problem of</u> online clothing size and fit, but there are, of course, many startups trying to use tech to solve the problem at source.
免運費是解決線上購物服飾尺寸和合身問題的一種方法，但當然也有很多新創公司嘗試利用科技從源頭解決這個問題。

tackle + issue　解決問題

Unfortunately, it seems the executives are not keen on <u>tackling the issue</u>. They are simply hoping it will go away.
不幸的是，高層主管似乎對於解決這個問題並不積極。他們只是希望問題會消失。

tackle + question　解決問題

The study did not <u>tackle the question of</u> whether this greenhouse effect will lead to global warming.
這項研究並沒有解決溫室效應是否會導致全球暖化的問題。

tackle + challenge　解決挑戰、難題

During the political campaign, candidates repeatedly promised to <u>tackle the challenge of</u> enhancing America's infrastructure.
在競選活動期間，候選人一再承諾會解決強化美國基礎設施的難題。

tackle + needs 解決需求

At present, no national scheme to <u>tackle the health needs of</u> all members of the veteran population exists.
目前，還沒有任何的國家計畫能解決所有退伍軍人的健康需求。

tackle + crime 解決犯罪問題

How to <u>tackle</u> drug-related <u>crimes</u> has been a challenge confronting many governments around the world.
如何打擊毒品犯罪一直都是世界各國政府面臨的挑戰。

tackle + unemployment 解決失業問題

If the government wants to <u>tackle unemployment</u>, it will have to carry out a thorough reform.
如果政府想要解決失業問題，就必須進行徹底改革。

tackle + poverty 解決貧困問題

The University of Michigan and Harvard University are teaming up to <u>tackle poverty</u> and drug addiction in Detroit.
密西根大學和哈佛大學正聯手解決底特律的貧困及藥物成癮的問題。

Take
▶ MP3-140
(take — took — taken)

take + break 休息一下

I'm not sure whether I should hand in my notice, but I do think it's time to <u>take a break</u>.

我不知道是否該辭職，但我確實認為是時候該休息一下了。

take + chance 冒險

After losing two million dollars on my previous business venture, I'm not <u>taking any chances</u> this time.

上次創業賠了 200 萬美元後，我這次不會再冒險了。

take + stand 表態、表明立場

Although many countries around the world are introducing booster shots against COVID-19 , the Union Government of India has yet to <u>take a stand on</u> the issue.

儘管世界上許多國家都開始施打 COVID-19 疫苗追加劑，印度政府仍未在這個議題上表態。

take + trip 去旅行

I recommend that you <u>take a trip</u> and take your mind off work to get a better idea of what is really going on.

我建議你去旅行、讓自己抽離工作，好釐清到底發生了什麼事。

A
B
C
D
E
F
G
H
I
J
K
L
M
N
O
P
Q
R
S
T
U
V
W

take + peek 偷看

Even though I don't drink, I often <u>take a peek</u> at the wine list to check out the prices.

雖然我不喝酒,但我常常會偷瞄酒單,看一下價格。

take + nap 小睡一下

Avoid long periods of driving after dark. Whenever you feel drowsy, find a safe spot to pull off the road and <u>take a nap</u>.

避免在夜晚長途駕駛。當你覺得昏昏欲睡時,找個安全的地方停下來小睡一下。

take + risk 冒險

Stepping outside of our comfort zone isn't easy. We have to muster up courage to <u>take a risk</u> and move past our personal limits.

跨出我們的舒適圈並不容易。我們必須鼓起勇氣去冒險,超越個人的極限。

take + time 需要時間

Doctors have told the family that it will <u>take time to</u> see whether that improves.

醫生告訴家屬,需要時間觀察情況是否改善。

take + initiative 積極主動

New hires should <u>take the initiative to</u> learn what will help them do their job better. That's what separates the person who excels from the person who winds up being stagnant.
新員工應該主動學習能幫助他們把工作做得更好的事。這就是優秀的人和停滯不前的人的差別。

take + medication / medicine 吃藥、服藥

I read online that people with heart problems should not <u>take this medicine</u>.
我在網路上看到有心臟問題的人不應該服用這種藥物。

take + lead 帶頭、率先

The global chip shortage problem continues. The industry has reported that TSMC, the global wafer leader, will <u>take the lead</u> and increase the foundry price by 20%.
全球晶片短缺的問題持續，據業界報導，全球晶圓龍頭台積電將率先調漲代工價格 20%。

實用短語 / 用法 / 句型

1. take the road less traveled 選擇一條較少人走過的路
Showing that you are willing to <u>take the road less traveled</u> is a way to show strength of character, a sign of a leader.
表現出你願意選擇一條較少人走過的路，這是展現個性優點的一種方式，也是領導者的象徵。

2. take a rain check 延期

I'm sorry but I'm busy on Saturday—can I <u>take a rain check</u>?

抱歉，我星期六很忙，我們可以改時間嗎？

3. take sb by surprise 使某人感到驚訝

The news that many firms in the U.S. have announced cuts this year <u>took me by surprise</u>.

美國今年有許多公司宣布裁員的消息讓我感到很驚訝。

Tell

▶ MP3-141

(tell — told — told)

tell + truth 說實話

At the time I thought he was exaggerating, but I was to discover that he was <u>telling the truth</u>.

當時我以為他講得太誇張，但後來我才發現他說的是實話。

tell + difference 區分差異

It's very difficult to <u>tell the difference between</u> real paintings and fake ones, but there are a few things we can look for to be sure.

真跡畫作和贗品很難區分，但我們可以從一些地方確認。

tell + story 講故事

Experts say GDP numbers won't give the answer but that they <u>tell</u> only <u>part of the story</u> instead.

專家表示，GDP 數字無法給出答案，它們只能說明部分情況。

tell + lie 說謊

The mayoral candidate accused his opponent of <u>telling a lie</u> together with city government officials about the market renovation project.

這位市長候選人指控他的對手與市政府官員聯手就市場改建工程一事說謊。

tell + joke 說笑話

When you feel that your students are falling asleep, <u>tell a joke</u>.
當你覺得你的學生快睡著了，就講個笑話吧。

實用短語 / 用法 / 句型

1. to tell you the truth 老實說

I didn't understand a lot of things they were doing, <u>to tell you the truth</u>.
老實說，他們做的很多事情我都不了解。

2. there is no telling 不知道、無法知道

We're fortunate we got the fire call. If it hadn't been for that call, <u>there is no telling</u> what would have happened to the building.
我們很幸運有接到火災通知。如果沒有那通電話，不知道這棟大樓會發生什麼事。

3. tell me about it 真的！（表示同意）

A: Assembling IKEA furniture is a lot of work.
　組裝 IKEA 的家具很費功夫。
B: <u>Tell me about it</u>! It took me three hours just to assemble a bedside table the other day.
　真的！前幾天我花了 3 個小時才組裝好一個床頭櫃。

Terminate

▶ MP3-142

(terminate — terminated — terminated)

terminate + contract 終止合約

At Tuesday's meeting, Allen again recommended that the council <u>terminate the contract</u> with the firm.
在週二的會議上，Allen 再次建議理事會終止與該公司的合約。

terminate + agreement 終止協議

We may <u>terminate this agreement</u>, if you breach any provision of these terms and conditions.
如果您違反這些條款和條件的任何規定，我們可能會終止此協議。

terminate + relationship 結束關係

Disconnection can often be the prelude to a decision to <u>terminate the relationship</u> or to pursue or act on a new love interest.
斷絕聯絡往往是決定結束關係、或是對新對象展開追求的前奏。

Throw

▶ MP3-143

(throw — threw — thrown)

throw + party 舉辦派對

We're <u>throwing a party</u> for Bill's retirement next week. Are you coming?
我們下週要幫 Bill 舉辦退休派對。你要來嗎？

throw + tantrum 發脾氣

Many children are surrounded by cellphones and tablets, and they often <u>throw a tantrum</u> when parents withhold their electronic devices.
很多孩子隨身帶著手機和平板電腦，當父母不給他們使用時，他們還經常大發脾氣。

throw + doubt 對～產生懷疑、質疑

Mr. Smith shocked the market with a joint statement that seemed to <u>throw doubt on</u> some of his predecessor's big decisions.
Smith 發表了一份聯合聲明震驚了市場，這份聲明似乎是對前任做的一些重大決策提出質疑。

throw + light 闡明、解釋

The study <u>throws a light on</u> various factors that influence our reactions to an adverse event.
這份研究解釋了影響我們產生不良反應的各種因素。

1. throw caution to the wind 不顧一切、豁出去了

I don't mind taking a little chance now and then, but I'm not the type of person who <u>throws caution to the wind</u>.

我不介意偶爾冒點險，但我不是那種會不顧一切豁出去的人。

2. throw one's money around 揮霍金錢

You can't just <u>throw money around</u> every month and expect to have enough left to pay the bills—you have to stick to your budget.

你不能每個月都亂花錢，還期待剩下的錢夠付帳單，你必須要遵守預算。

3. throw a fit 大發脾氣

When he started <u>throwing a fit</u> in the department store, everyone was looking at us and I was so embarrassed.

當他開始在百貨公司大發脾氣時，每個人都看著我們，我超級尷尬。

4. throw sb into confusion 使人陷入混亂

The company <u>was thrown into confusion</u> by the sudden resignations of several top-level officials.

幾位高層主管突然辭職，使公司陷入混亂。

A
B
C
D
E
F
G
H
I
J
K
L
M
N
O
P
Q
R
S
T
U
V
W

Thwart

(thwart — thwarted — thwarted)

thwart + attempts 阻撓嘗試

Saudi Arabia has <u>thwarted attempts to</u> smuggle drugs into the country and arrested 50 suspects.
沙烏地阿拉伯阻止了走私毒品進該國的企圖，並逮捕了 50 名嫌犯。

thwart + efforts 阻撓努力

Politicians who have attempted to <u>thwart the efforts to</u> cooperate with other Asian countries have been widely criticized.
那些試圖阻撓我們與其他亞洲國家合作的政客，受到來自四面八方的批評。

thwart + plans 阻撓計畫、計畫泡湯

The COVID-19 pandemic has <u>thwarted</u> the company's <u>plan</u> to open more factories in the U.S.
COVID-19 阻礙了這間公司在美國增設工廠的計畫。

thwart + development 阻礙發展

These drugs may <u>thwart the development of</u> protective immune mechanisms, and it is recommended that they be used with caution.
這些藥物可能會阻礙保護性免疫機制的發展，建議謹慎使用。

Tighten

▶ MP3-145

(tighten — tightened — tightened)

tighten + rules 加強規定、使法規更嚴格

If governments <u>tighten rules</u>, they could make it harder for the firm to carry on minting money from ads.

如果各國政府加強法規,他們可能會使這間公司更難繼續利用廣告賺錢。

tighten + security 加強安全措施

In the wake of the death of a second-grader at her school, Taipei's Department of Education said it will take emergency measures to <u>tighten</u> the school's <u>security</u>.

一名二年級孩童在學校遇害後,臺北市教育局表示將採取緊急措施,加強校園安全。

實用短語 / 用法 / 句型

1. tighten one's belt 勒緊褲帶、省吃儉用

The outbreak of COVID-19 has forced domestic service enterprises to <u>tighten their belts</u> as customers disappear.

隨著顧客減少,COVID-19 疫情的爆發使國內服務業不得不減少支出。

2. tighten the reins 加強管控

I wish those parents would <u>tighten the reins on</u> their kids. The little devils are tearing this restaurant apart!

我真希望那些父母能對他們的孩子們更嚴一點。這些小惡魔快要把餐廳拆了！

3. tighten the screws 施加壓力

The bank has really started <u>tightening the screws on</u> me ever since I began missing my mortgage payments.

自從我開始拖欠房貸後，銀行就開始對我施加壓力。

Uncover

(uncover — uncovered — uncovered)

uncover + truth　揭露真相

As she tried to <u>uncover the truth</u>, she put herself in mortal danger.
當她試圖揭露真相時,她使自己陷入了致命的危險。

uncover + secrets　揭露祕密

The Social Animal combines neuroscience with philosophy to <u>uncover the secrets of</u> happiness.
《社交動物》（The Social Animal）一書結合神經科學與哲學,揭開了幸福的祕密。

uncover + reasons　揭露原因

The study <u>uncovered the reasons</u> people do not donate or recycle clothing, with 49% saying they did not think they could because the clothes were worn out or dirty.
這項研究揭露了人們不捐贈或回收衣物的原因,49% 的人表示,他們認為無法捐贈或回收,因為衣服都已經破舊或髒了。

uncover + plot　揭露陰謀

They were given 24-hour police protection after <u>the plot was uncovered</u>.
在陰謀被揭露後,他們受到警方 24 小時的保護。

uncover + potential 發掘潛力

The status quo will not bring about the innovation necessary to <u>uncover the full potential of</u> your team.

現狀不會帶來創新來發掘你的團隊全部潛力。

Undermine

▶ MP3-147

(undermine — undermined — undermined)

undermine + credibility 破壞信譽、可信度

This party has been attempting to disrupt preventive efforts taken by Taiwan against the coronavirus and spreading fake news to <u>undermine the credibility of</u> the nation's medical leaders.
這個政黨一直試圖破壞臺灣對新冠病毒的防疫工作，並散播假新聞來破壞國家醫界領袖的信譽。

undermine + integrity 破壞公正性

Sports wagering has the potential to <u>undermine the integrity of</u> sports contests and jeopardize the well-being of student athletes.
運動博弈有可能會破壞體育競賽的公正性，並危害學生運動員的福祉。

undermine + ability 削弱能力

Such a ban would hurt business and <u>undermine the ability to</u> serve customers who come to the sites to drink.
這樣的禁令會影響生意，也使店家無法服務來喝酒的顧客。

undermine + effectiveness 損害有效性

Millions of people are at risk if variants are more transmissible, more deadly and more likely to <u>undermine the effectiveness of</u> current vaccines.

如果變種病毒更容易傳播、更致命、而且更有可能損害現行疫苗的有效性，那麼數百萬人都處於危險之中。

undermine + efforts 破壞、毀了努力

The politician's inappropriate words would threaten to <u>undermine the efforts</u> that our country and people have made for democracy over the past two decades.

這位政客的不當言論，可能會毀了我們國家和人民在過去 20 年為民主所做的努力。

undermine + confidence 削弱信心

Russian intelligence agencies have attempted to <u>undermine confidence in</u> Western vaccines, using articles that have questioned the vaccines' development and safety.

俄羅斯情報機構試圖利用質疑疫苗研發和安全性的文章，削弱人們對西方疫苗的信心。

Underscore

▶ MP3-148

(underscore — underscored — underscored)

underscore + importance 強調重要性

We <u>underscore the importance of</u> peace and stability across the Taiwan Strait and encourage the peaceful resolution of cross-Strait issues.
我們強調臺海和平穩定的重要性，鼓勵和平解決兩岸問題。

underscore + need 強調需求

The findings <u>underscore the need to</u> seek more economic diversity during difficult and uncertain times.
研究結果強調，在艱困、充滿變化的時期，需要尋求更多的經濟多樣性。

underscore + value 強調價值

Researchers said the findings <u>underscore the value of</u> physical exercise, healthy diets and weight loss.
研究人員表示，這些研究結果強調了運動、健康飲食和減重的價值。

underscore + necessity 強調必要性

The COVID-19 pandemic has <u>underscored the necessity of</u> a comprehensive healthcare system.
COVID-19 凸顯了健全醫療體系的必要性。

Unlock

(unlock — unlocked — unlocked)

unlock + potential 激發潛力

The coffee chain has already managed to <u>unlock the potential of</u> mobile payments. So far, its app has chalked up 60 million transactions.

這家連鎖咖啡店成功激發了行動支付的潛力。到目前為止，它的應用程式已完成 6,000 萬筆交易。

unlock + power 釋放力量

Our company has been committed to <u>unlocking the power of</u> data, hoping to leverage data analytics to help companies know more about their potential customers.

我們公司一直致力於解鎖數據，希望利用數據分析來幫助企業更了解他們的潛在客戶。

unlock + secrets 解開祕密

People interested in digital marketing today are all trying hard to <u>unlock the secrets of</u> Google's search algorithm.

現今對數位行銷有興趣的人，都在努力解開 Google 搜尋演算法的祕密。

Unpack

▶ MP3-150

(unpack — unpacked — unpacked)

unpack + box 打開箱子

For your safety, you should carefully examine whether <u>the box</u> has been opened by anyone before you <u>unpack</u> it.
為了您的安全，在您開箱前請仔細檢查箱子是否有被拆開過。

unpack + concept 解釋概念

In this discussion I shall try to <u>unpack the concept of</u> the metaverse in order to phrase its importance in broader terms.
在這次的討論中，為了更廣泛說明元宇宙的重要性，我會嘗試解釋它的概念。

unpack + meaning 解釋意義

We probably need legal counsel to <u>unpack the meaning of</u> this document for us.
我們可能需要法律顧問來為我們解釋這份文件的意思。

A
B
C
D
E
F
G
H
I
J
K
L
M
N
O
P
Q
R
S
T
U
V
W

Unravel

(unravel — unraveled — unraveled)

unravel + mystery 解開謎團

In this week's episode, we are going to find out how experts are trying to <u>unravel the mystery of</u> who appears to be at more risk of contracting COVID-19.

在本週的節目中,我們將一探專家是如何試圖解開哪些人較容易感染 COVID-19 的謎團。

unravel + complexities 解開複雜性

Since my mother died of cancer 29 years ago, scientists working to <u>unravel the complexities of</u> cancer and find new therapies are my heroes.

自從 29 年前我母親死於癌症後,那些致力於解開癌症複雜性並尋找新療法的科學家就是我的英雄。

Unveil

▶ MP3-152

(unveil — unveiled — unveiled)

unveil + plans 公布計畫

The administration is expected to <u>unveil its plans for</u> reforms in healthcare finance early next year.
預計政府將在明年初公布醫療照護的財務改革計畫。

unveil + results 公布結果

Mercedes-Benz has <u>unveiled the results of</u> an 18-month project to develop the next generation of luxury EVs—the Vision EQXX.
賓士公布了一項為期 18 個月的計畫成果，這項計畫是開發下一代的豪華電動車 Vision EQXX。

unveil + secrets 揭開祕密

The successful landing of the Mars rover has led to great expectations within the world's scientific community. Many are hoping for the chance to <u>unveil the secrets of</u> Mars.
火星探測器的成功著陸，讓全球科學界抱有很大的期待，許多人都希望有機會揭開火星的祕密。

A
B
C
D
E
F
G
H
I
J
K
L
M
N
O
P
Q
R
S
T
U
V
W

實用短語 / 用法 / 句型

1. unveil the latest version of sth 推出最新版本

Apple is widely expected to <u>unveil the latest version of</u> its MacBook Pro, which is rumored to feature the M1X processor.

外界普遍預期，蘋果將推出新款 MacBook Pro，據傳將搭載 M1X 處理器。

Uphold
(uphold — upheld — upheld)

▶ MP3-153

uphold + law 維護法律

He received the harsh sentence due to the seriousness
of the crime, and because he had a great responsibility to
<u>uphold the law</u> as a former police officer.
他因罪行嚴重，且身為一名前警員、身負維護法律的重任，而被判
處重刑。

uphold + principles 堅持原則

Overcoming inner prejudice may be one of the hardest
behavioral <u>principles</u> to <u>uphold</u>.
克服內心的偏見可能是最難堅持的行為原則之一。

uphold + decision 維持決定

There is no indication as of yet whether the Biden
administration will <u>uphold the decision of</u> the former
government and put it into practice.
目前沒有跡象顯示，拜登政府是否會維持前任政府的決定並付諸實行。

uphold + standards 維持標準

We take seriously our responsibility to <u>uphold the highest</u>
health and safety <u>standards</u> that protect Taiwan's food supply.
我們認真履行維護臺灣食品供應的最高健康與安全標準的責任。

Upset

▶ MP3-154

(upset — upset — upset)

upset + stomach 使胃感到不舒服

Foods that may <u>upset your stomach</u>, such as fatty, fried or spicy foods, are best avoided before sleep.
睡前最好避免吃一些可能會讓你胃不舒服的食物，例如油膩、油炸或是辛辣的東西。

upset + balance 破壞平衡

We have <u>upset the balance of</u> nature. It's time for us to strike a balance between our climate change commitments and the need for economic stimulus packages.
我們破壞了大自然的平衡。是時候該在氣候變遷承諾和經濟刺激方案之間取得平衡。

upset + status quo 打破現狀

The Chinese Minister of Foreign Affairs said the US and other countries were trying to <u>upset the status quo in</u> Beijing's relations with Taiwan.
中國外交部長表示，美國和其他國家試圖破壞北京與臺灣關係的現狀。

實用短語 / 用法 / 句型

1. upset the apple cart 打亂計畫

It will only <u>upset the apple cart</u> and confuse the issue if the topic is raised too soon.

如果太早提出這個議題，只會打亂計畫、讓問題變得混亂。

Utilize

(utilize — utilized — utilized)

utilize + technology 利用科技

To <u>utilize technology in</u> teaching and increase the nation's competitiveness, the government has built 42,966 smart-learning classrooms.
為了將科技運用在教學當中並提高國家競爭力,政府已經打造了 42,966 間智慧學習教室。

utilize + information 利用資訊

Smart cities <u>utilize information</u> and communication technology to improve operational efficiency, share information with the public, and provide a better quality of government service.
智慧城市利用資訊和通訊科技來提高營運效率,與民眾共享資訊、並提供更優質的政府服務。

utilize + multimedia 利用多媒體

These user data are useful for companies seeking to <u>utilize multimedia</u> to advertise and market their products.
這些使用者數據對於尋求利用多媒體來宣傳和行銷產品的公司很有用。

utilize + resources 利用資源

While our platform gives you access to a huge library of photos, you can always <u>utilize resources</u> such as YouTube and other sites.

雖然我們的平台給您龐大的圖庫可作使用，但您仍可以隨時利用 YouTube 和其他網站的資源。

utilize + abilities 利用能力

The question of how the organization can change to better <u>utilize the abilities</u> and knowledge <u>of</u> every talent has not been addressed.

關於組織要如何改變，來更充分利用每個人才的能力和知識，這個問題還沒有被解決。

utilize + services 利用服務

The most efficient solution to your problem is to <u>utilize the services of</u> a mental health professional.

解決你問題最有效的方法，是利用心理健康專業人員的服務。

Vaccinate

▶ MP3-156

(vaccinate — vaccinated — vaccinated)

實用短語 / 用法 / 句型

1. get vaccinated against sth 接種～疫苗

Public health officials recommend that everyone aged 12 and up <u>get vaccinated against</u> COVID-19, including those who were previously infected.

公共衛生官員建議所有 12 歲（含）以上的人接種 COVID-19 疫苗，包括之前已確診過的人。

Vary

▶ MP3-157

(vary — varied — varied)

實用短語 / 用法 / 句型

1. vary from sth to sth 因～而異

Ticket prices <u>vary from</u> tour <u>to</u> tour and site <u>to</u> site but are usually under $50.
票價會因路線和地點而有所不同，但通常不超過 50 美元。

2. vary depending on sth 因～而異

Glamping typically costs NT$6,000 to $10,000 per day, which includes a tent, board and activities. Rates will <u>vary depending on</u> the activities, meals and the tent you choose.
豪華露營通常一天是新臺幣 6,000 至 10,000 元，包含帳篷、食宿、和活動。價格將根據您選擇的活動、餐點、和帳篷而有所不同。

3. vary according to sth 因～而異

Cancellation and prepayment policies <u>vary according to</u> accommodations type. Please enter the dates of your stay and check what conditions apply to your preferred room.
取消訂房和訂金的規定因房型而異，請輸入您的入住日期，並查看適用於您所選客房的條件。

Violate

▶ MP3-158

(violate — violated — violated)

violate + copyright 侵犯版權

Even if you give the copyright owner credit, posting images that you don't purchase may still <u>violate copyright</u>.
即使你有標示版權所有者，發布你未購買的圖片仍可能侵犯版權。

violate + law 違反法律

Businesses that knowingly <u>violate the law</u> could have their operating licenses revoked.
故意違反法律的企業可能會被撤銷營業執照。

violate + standards 違反標準

Any pet food suppliers who <u>violate the standards</u> could be fined NT$50,000 to NT$250,000 based on the magnitude of the damage.
任何違反標準的寵物食品供應商，將依損害程度，處以新臺幣 5 萬至 25 萬元的罰款。

violate + rights 侵犯權利

Some activists say the measures <u>violate human rights</u> because they only target migrant workers.
一些社會運動人士説，這些措施侵犯了人權，因為它們只針對移工。

violate + rules 違反規定

Action will be taken against users who repeatedly <u>violate our rules</u> on things like hate speech.

對於多次違反我們仇恨言論等規定的用戶，我們將採取行動。

Voice

▶ MP3-159

(voice — voiced — voiced)

voice + opinion 發表意見

Come join our live podcast tonight to <u>voice your opinion</u> or ask questions during the show.
快加入我們今晚的 podcast 直播，在節目中發表你的意見或提問。

voice + support 表達支持

I cordially invite all of you to join us tomorrow, to <u>voice your support for</u> Taiwan's membership in the WHO.
我誠摯邀請大家明天加入我們，表達你對臺灣加入世界衛生組織的支持。

voice + concerns 表達擔憂

The students met with lawmakers after the news conference to <u>voice their concerns about</u> tuition hikes.
新聞記者會後，學生們與立法委員會面，表達了他們對學費調漲的擔憂。

voice + opposition 表達反對

Environmentalists are urging residents to call their local lawmakers to <u>voice opposition to</u> the budget cuts.
環保人士呼籲居民打電話給當地議員，表達對預算刪減的反對。

Waive

▶ MP3-160

(waive — waived — waived)

waive + requirement 放棄要求

The administration would <u>waive the requirement to</u> have a certain balance at the end of the budget to cover unexpected expenses.
政府將放棄保留一定的預算餘額來支付意外費用的這個要求。

waive + fees 免除費用

The airlines said it will <u>waive fees</u> it would normally charge for changing travel plans.
航空公司表示，將免除因更改旅程而收取的費用。

waive + payment 免除費用

Putting the interests of our students first, we have decided to <u>waive the payment</u> for accommodations provided by the University from March 20 for all students.
我們以學生利益為重，決定從 3 月 20 日起免除所有學生的住宿費。

waive + right 放棄權利

Many schools require students to <u>waive their right to</u> view letters of recommendation as part of the application process.
許多學校在申請過程中，要求學生放棄查看推薦信的權利。

A
B
C
D
E
F
G
H
I
J
K
L
M
N
O
P
Q
R
S
T
U
V
W

Walk

▶ MP3-161

(walk — walked — walked)

walk + dog 遛狗

I used to live right next to the harbor and <u>walk my dog</u> along the waterfront every morning and night.
我以前就住在港口旁邊，每天早晚都會沿著海濱遛狗。

實用短語 / 用法 / 句型

1. walk sb home 送某人回家、陪某人走回家

Let me make you a fresh cup of coffee and then I'll <u>walk you home</u>.
我幫你煮杯咖啡，然後送你回家。

2. walk the talk 說到做到、付諸行動

To create a productive organizational culture, the top leader has to <u>walk the talk</u> and be the role model.
要創造高效的組織文化，高層主管必須說到做到、作為榜樣。

3. walk the walk 說到做到、付諸行動

What we have to do is really <u>walk the walk</u> and not just talk the talk.
我們要說到做到，不能只是光說不練。

4. walk on eggshells 小心謹慎

When it comes to weight issues, parents should <u>walk on eggshells</u> while talking to teenagers.
和青少年聊到體重時，父母要小心說話。

Wane

▶ MP3-162

(wane — waned — waned)

interest + wane 興趣、關注減弱

Special discounts will certainly boost sales through the upcoming holiday but <u>interest</u> might <u>wane</u> after the holiday spending season.

特價肯定會在即將到來的假期間刺激銷售，但在這個購物檔期過後，顧客的興趣可能會減弱。

enthusiasm + wane 熱情減退

It's normal to find that your <u>enthusiasm</u> waxes and <u>wanes</u> when you're pursing a long-term goal.

追求長期目標的過程中，你發現你的熱情會起起伏伏是很正常的。

influence + wane 影響減弱

As Tim Cook asserted a more cost-conscious approach to new products, the designer's <u>influence</u> began to <u>wane</u>.

隨著 Tim Cook 主張對新產品採用更注重成本控管的做法，這位設計師的影響力開始減弱。

support + wane 支持減弱

People's <u>support</u> will surely <u>wane</u> if parliament proves to be as toothless as it has been over the past month.

如果議會證實像過去一個月一樣沒用，民眾對它的支持肯定會減弱。

popularity + wane 人氣下滑、支持度下降

Three prime ministers have been ousted by their own party since 2010 after their <u>popularity</u> began to <u>wane</u>.

自 2010 年以來，已經有三位部長在支持度下降後被自己的政黨趕下台。

Withdraw

▶ MP3-163

(withdraw — withdrew — withdrawn)

withdraw + troops 撤軍

The new president has vowed to <u>withdraw troops from</u> Iraq within 16 months.
新任總統誓言要在 16 個月內從伊拉克撤軍。

withdraw + money 領錢、提款

It is strongly recommended that you apply for an ATM card, so you can use it to <u>withdraw money from</u> ATMs anytime.
強烈建議你申請一張提款卡，這樣就可以隨時用它在自動櫃員機提款。

withdraw + support 收回支持

Sandy <u>withdrew her support for</u> the candidate after finding out that he was against same-sex marriage.
Sandy 發現自己支持的候選人反對同性婚姻後，收回了對他的支持。

withdraw + funding 收回資金

President Donald Trump announced Friday he would <u>withdraw funding from</u> the World Health Organization.
總統 Donald Trump 週五宣布，他將收回對世界衛生組織的資助。

實用短語 / 用法 / 句型

1. withdraw from the competition 退出比賽

In a statement, tournament organizers confirmed that Novak Djokovic has <u>withdrawn from the competition</u>.
在一份聲明中，巡迴賽主辦方證實 Novak Djokovic 已經退出比賽。

2. withdraw from public life 退出公眾生活

In 2010, she <u>withdrew from public life</u> suffering from Alzheimer's disease.
2010 年，她因罹患阿茲海默症而退出了公眾生活。

3. withdraw from the market 退出市場

Safety concerns arose almost four years before the drug <u>was withdrawn from the market</u>.
在這個藥品退出市場的近 4 年前，人們對其安全性早有疑慮。

memo

國家圖書館出版品預行編目資料

搭配詞的力量 Collocations：動詞篇 / 王梓沅著
-- 初版 -- 臺北市：瑞蘭國際，2022.08
384 面；14.8×21 公分 --（外語達人系列；24）
ISBN：978-986-5560-81-2（平裝）
1.CST：英語 2.CST：動詞

805.165   111011782

外語達人系列 24

搭配詞的力量 動詞篇
Collocations

作者｜王梓沅．作者助理｜胡嘉修．責任編輯｜葉仲芸、王愿琦
校對｜王梓沅、胡嘉修、葉仲芸、王愿琦

英語錄音｜Terri Lynn Pebsworth
錄音室｜采漾錄音製作有限公司
封面設計｜蔡嘉恩．版型設計｜陳如琪．內文排版｜邱亭瑜

瑞蘭國際出版
董事長｜張暖彗．社長兼總編輯｜王愿琦
編輯部
副總編輯｜葉仲芸．主編｜潘治婷
設計部主任｜陳如琪
業務部
經理｜楊米琪．主任｜林湲洵．組長｜張毓庭

出版社｜瑞蘭國際有限公司．地址｜台北市大安區安和路一段 104 號 7 樓之 1
電話｜(02)2700-4625．傳真｜(02)2700-4622．訂購專線｜(02)2700-4625
劃撥帳號｜19914152 瑞蘭國際有限公司．瑞蘭國際網路書城｜www.genki-japan.com.tw

法律顧問｜海灣國際法律事務所　呂錦峯律師

總經銷｜聯合發行股份有限公司．電話｜(02)2917-8022、2917-8042
傳真｜(02)2915-6275、2915-7212．印刷｜科億印刷股份有限公司
出版日期｜2022 年 08 月初版 1 刷．定價｜480 元．ISBN｜978-986-5560-81-2
　　　　　2023 年 07 月初版 2 刷

瑞蘭國際